I0763673

THE MARKED

Book #4

Of the

The Moores Hill Thriller Series

by

Ray Brown

COPYRIGHT

The MARKED

Published by Human Perimeter Press™
An Imprint of SentriPup Labs, LLC

ISBN: 979-8-9939776-6-9

Okeana, Ohio USA

First Edition: June 1, 2026

Chief Editor: Karen Fox, Human Perimeter Press™

Cover design by Human Perimeter Press™

DEDICATION

To the nearby communities of St. Leon, Dover,

New Alsace, and Yorkville.

You held the line. You came together as one.

And on the day that it mattered most, it was enough.

TABLE OF CONTENTS

AUTHOR'S NOTE

The Marked is a work of fiction. The town of Moores Hill is real. The characters are not. But the crisis at the center of this story -- a prolonged regional electrical grid failure affecting millions of Americans simultaneously -- is not a scenario I invented for dramatic effect. It is a scenario that infrastructure engineers, emergency management professionals, and federal planners have been modeling, studying, and warning about for decades.

The American electrical grid is, by the assessment of the people responsible for protecting it, one of the most vulnerable pieces of critical infrastructure in the developed world. It was not designed as a single unified system. It grew organically over more than a century through thousands of separate decisions made by hundreds of separate utility companies operating under fragmented regulatory oversight. The result is a patchwork of aging infrastructure carrying loads it was never designed to carry, increasingly strained by the power demands of data centers, cryptocurrency mining operations, and the electrification of systems that previously ran on other energy sources.

The backup transformer capacity that protects regional grid stability is largely manufactured overseas. Lead times run fourteen to eighteen months under normal conditions. The United States does not maintain a strategic reserve of large high-voltage transformers. A coordinated attack on transformer infrastructure, or a cascade failure triggered by sustained overload at vulnerable interconnection points, would produce outages measured not in hours or days but in months.

This is not speculation. This is the documented assessment of the Federal Emergency Management Agency, the Department of Energy, and the President's National Infrastructure Advisory Council, whose 2018 report on prolonged power outage described a scenario almost identical to the one depicted in this novel and concluded that the consequences would be, in their language, catastrophic and potentially irreversible for the affected population.

FEMA's own planning frameworks acknowledge that civil order in urban areas begins to deteriorate within seventy-two hours of a major disaster when residents exhaust their immediate supplies. In a localized disaster a hurricane, a flood, an earthquake, help arrives from outside the affected area. In a prolonged regional grid failure affecting multiple states simultaneously, there is no outside. Every community in the region is managing the same shortage simultaneously.

Under those conditions, FEMA's modeling suggests that the organized movement of urban populations toward rural areas with food and water resources begins within the first two to three weeks. It begins as individual movement and becomes collective movement as people discover others are moving in the same direction for the same reasons. Collective movement, under sustained resource pressure, becomes something harder to characterize and harder to manage.

The events depicted at the St. Leon I-74 interchange in this novel occur approximately five weeks into the outage. By the documented modeling of the agencies responsible for American emergency preparedness, that timeline is conservative. The St. Leon scenario is not a dramatic invention. It is a projection that emergency planners have explicitly modeled and that historians of disaster have documented in analogous events in other countries and other centuries.

I did not write The Marked to frighten anyone. I wrote it because Moores Hill is a real place and the people who live in communities like it are real people, and the question of what those communities would do and who they would become under conditions of sustained catastrophic stress is one of the most genuinely interesting questions I know how to ask.

The answer this novel offers is not pessimistic. The people of Moores Hill are not heroes in any extraordinary sense. They are ordinary people making ordinary decisions with the materials available to them. What the research consistently shows is that small communities with strong social networks and existing relationships of trust outperform larger populations in prolonged crisis scenarios by a significant margin.

Moores Hill survives, to the extent that it survives, not because its people are exceptional. Because they know each other.

That, at least, is something we can all work on before we need it.

Ray Brown
Human Perimeter Press

PROLOGUE

THE SHEEP

The Irish Bowl burned on a Tuesday.

Emma was not there. She was not yet born when it happened. But some events leave marks on the places where they occur that outlast every witness. The Irish Bowl was that kind of event. You could feel it in Moores Hill if you knew where to press. A bruise that never fully healed. A silence that fell in certain conversations. The particular look on the faces of people who had been there that morning and had never fully found the words for what they saw.

In her dream she found the words.

The storm had come through the night before. The kind that announces itself with stillness first, the air going green and heavy in the late afternoon, and then arriving with the full weight of everything it had been building. Trees down. Power lines pulled low by fallen timber, sagging to places they were never designed to reach. At the intersection of Route 350 and Main Street the lines had come down nearly to shoulder height. Nobody had gotten to them yet. It was early. The town was just waking up.

The delivery truck driver did not know.

He pulled into the Shell station with his load the way he had pulled into a hundred stations before it. Routine. Ordinary. The kind of morning move that requires no thought. And in Emma's dream she could see it happening with the terrible slow clarity of nightmares, could see the load was too high, could see the lines were too low, could see exactly what was about to happen and could not stop it and could not look away.

The sound the lines made when they caught was not an explosion. Not yet. It was something worse. A sound that lived below hearing and above feeling, a frequency that bypassed the ears entirely and arrived directly in the chest. The stretched groan of power that had been contained for decades suddenly finding a path it was never meant to travel.

And then the first transformer blew.

The concussion hit Emma before the sound did. A physical force, a wall of pressure that arrived faster than physics should allow, and in its wake something that should not have been possible.

The demon ball.

There was no other name for it. No natural explanation that covered what she was seeing. A sphere of fire and electrical force, blue-white at its core and surrounded by a corona that her dreaming mind could not assign a color to, hovering for one suspended moment at the site of the first transformer before it chose a direction.

It chose down the line.

It moved.

Not the way fire moves, consuming what is nearest, spreading outward in all directions with the democratic hunger of combustion. This moved with purpose. This moved the way a predator moves when it has already identified its target and the only remaining question is pace. Transformer after transformer detonating in sequence as it passed, each explosion feeding it, each explosion announcing its progress down nearly a mile of Moores Hill's power infrastructure while the town watched from porches and sidewalks and the windows of houses that were already losing their lights.

The sound built into something that had no business existing in southern Indiana on a Tuesday morning. Not a fire. Not a storm. A war. A bombardment. The kind of sound that belongs to places where history is being made by force and people are helpless before it.

It found the Irish Bowl.

Of course it did. Emma understood in the dream what she could not have articulated while awake. The demon ball had not been traveling randomly. It had not been seeking the nearest conductor or the weakest point in the line. It had been seeking the heart of the town. The place where Moores Hill had been most itself for decades. The lanes and the pins and the scorecards and the Friday nights and the birthday parties and the league standings posted on the wall by the front desk where at least one of the brothers John, Shorty, or Jim McClanahan had worked every evening for thirty years.

The 440 volts that fed the pin machines was not fuel. It was an invitation. The demon ball arrived and the electrical infrastructure of the Irish Bowl answered and what followed was not a fire in any sense that the fire department standing directly behind the building had trained for.

They were there. Emma could see them in the dream. Professional. Equipped. Present. Everything they needed to fight a fire arrayed and ready behind a building that was already beyond fire.

They could not go forward. The heat coming off the structure was not the heat of burning wood or burning insulation. It was the heat of raw voltage freed from every constraint, the heat of electricity doing what electricity does when no one and nothing is controlling it anymore, and it was cooking the air itself at a distance that made their equipment meaningless. They stood at the edge of what was survivable and watched.

The Irish Bowl burned.

It burned with a completeness that Emma in her dream understood was not accidental. The kind of burning that is not content to destroy but must also erase. When it was over, when the demon ball had finally exhausted itself and the voltage had found its way to ground and the fire department could finally move forward into what remained, Emma walked to where the walls had been.

She touched the ash with her foot.

It disintegrated. Not crumbled. Not broke apart. Disintegrated. What had been brick, what had been the solid constructed evidence of a community's investment in itself, was now nothing. Less than nothing. The fire had burned so completely and so hot that the material world had simply surrendered to it.

She understood what Moores Hill had understood that morning.

This was not an accident that had happened to a building. The demon ball had traveled nearly a mile of Indiana power lines and it had found the heart of this community and it had burned it to ash so thorough that brick could not survive it. This was the heart extinguished. The league nights and the Friday evenings and the sound of pins falling and everyone knowing everyone, gone. Not damaged. Not diminished.

Gone.

As if something had decided Moores Hill needed to be brought low.

As if the town was being punished.

Emma woke with that feeling still in her chest like a coal that had not finished burning.

She was soaked through. Hair. Clothes. Pillow. Everything. Rufus was pressed against her with an urgency she had only seen in him a handful of times, his whole body communicating the single message that something was wrong and she needed to come back and she needed to come back now.

She put her hand on him. Breathed.

Reached for the light switch.

Nothing.

Checked her phone. No signal. 4:38 AM.

She went to the window. Carnegie Hall's bell tower stood against the pre-dawn sky. Dark. The lights that illuminated it every night were gone. Main Street was dark in every direction. No streetlights. No porch lights. No glow from a single window in any direction.

The town was dark the way it had been dark before anyone thought to run wires through it.

The grid was down.

Emma stood at the window with Rufus pressed against her leg and the Irish Bowl still smoldering somewhere in the back of her mind and understood that Moores Hill was about to find out again what it felt like when something larger than itself decided it needed to be brought low.

She went to find her emergency kit.

THE WOLF

Robert Caldwell's monitoring systems were going dark.

One by one. Access point by access point. The window into American databases that he had spent twenty plus years building and refining and protecting closing sequentially, each access point going silent as the Midwestern grid took down the servers he had been quietly routing through. He watched it happen in real time and could not stop it. Could not reroute fast enough. The digital infrastructure was going dark the way lights go dark in a building you can see from across the street but cannot enter.

The missing persons database first. Then the property records. Then the Forest Service incident reports. Then the financial monitoring systems. Then everything.

He could see perfectly. He was completely blind.

He sat with his coffee going cold and the Peruvian night going about its business outside his window and thought about the work he had been building toward for two decades. The network. The families. The convergence he believed was coming in his lifetime and had organized his entire existence around facilitating.

All of it dependent on access he no longer had.

And the last thing he had seen before the American grid took it all offline was a fragment. An incomplete query result from the missing persons database, cached in his system before the connection dropped. Someone else had been running the same search he ran. Keyed to the same coordinates. Using a slightly different methodology but asking the same essential question.

Someone had been looking for the same things he had been looking for.

Someone had found his ghost pattern.

He sat in the dark of his own making, surrounded by Peruvian night, and turned that fragment over in his mind with the particular focused attention of a man who has learned over twenty years that the details that feel like coincidence are never coincidence.

Someone knew he existed.

He did not yet know who.

He would find out.

CHAPTER 1: THE LIGHTS GO OUT

Nobody owned the American electrical grid.

This was not a secret. It was simply a fact that most Americans never had occasion to think about, the way most Americans never thought about the structural condition of the bridges they drove across every day. The grid existed. It worked. That was the extent of the relationship most people had with it, and that relationship had been sufficient for decades because the grid, for all its age and patchwork construction, had kept working.

It was not one system. It was thousands of systems, owned and operated by hundreds of separate utility companies, connected through a web of transmission agreements and shared infrastructure and regulatory frameworks whose authority had never quite caught up with the reality of what they were supposed to oversee. The federal government had opinions about the grid. Multiple agencies had opinions about the grid. None of them had the authority to compel the changes that engineers had been recommending, with increasing urgency, for the better part of thirty years.

The grid had been built for a different country. One whose fundamental assumptions about what electricity was for and how much of it Americans would need had not survived contact with the twenty-first century.

The first pressure was simply time. Infrastructure that is not replaced eventually fails. Transformers designed for a forty-year service life were running at fifty and sixty, their insulation degrading, their tolerances shrinking, their capacity to handle unexpected load diminishing with each year they ran past their design specifications. Replacing them was expensive. Utilities had shareholders. The math of deferred maintenance is always attractive in the short term and catastrophic in the long one, and American utility companies had been making the short-term calculation for decades.

The second pressure arrived faster than anyone had predicted. The new generation of data centers required by artificial intelligence development consumed electricity the way industrial smelters consumed it, drawing hundreds of megawatts continuously, not in the variable patterns of residential or commercial users but in the sustained flat-line demand of machines that did not sleep and did not recognize the concept of off-peak hours. Three such facilities had come online in the Midwest in the eighteen months before the Tuesday in June when everything stopped. Each had been approved. Each had been connected to the grid with the full knowledge of the utility companies whose infrastructure served them. What those companies had not done, because no single entity had the authority to compel them to do it together, was coordinate the combined impact of three facilities of this scale coming online in the same regional grid sector within the same eighteen-month window.

The backup transformer capacity the expansion required had been ordered. The delivery date was eight months out. The facilities could not wait eight months

The third pressure was quieter still. Bitcoin mining operations had been arriving in the Midwest for years, drawn by cheap electricity and accommodating regulatory environments. A large mining facility looked, from the outside, like any other industrial building. Unlike a city, it had no natural load variation. It ran flat. Full capacity, all hours, every day, with the impassive consistency of machines pursuing a single objective with no awareness of the system around them.

Nobody had added up all three pressures in the same calculation. Not officially. Engineers had done it privately and shared the results in conversations at industry conferences and in emails carefully worded to avoid saying directly what they were saying. The grid was not a system that could be fixed by any single decision from any single authority, because no single authority existed. It was the sum of thousands of separate decisions made by hundreds of separate entities over decades, each one locally rational and collectively catastrophic.

This was the system that a small cell of men found when they began looking for vulnerabilities in American infrastructure.

What they found surprised even them.

They had expected a target requiring significant technical sophistication to damage. What they found instead was a system that had been doing the damage to itself for thirty years and required only the right pressure at the right points to finish what it had started. The switching stations where the new AI cluster connections met the existing infrastructure. The points where the load was heaviest and the backup capacity was absent and the tolerance for additional strain had already been consumed by time and deferred maintenance.

They introduced failures at those points.

The grid does not fail all at once. It fails in sequence, each overloaded sector pushing its excess load onto adjacent sectors already carrying more than they were designed for, the cascade moving through the interconnected system with the momentum of a failure that has nothing structural to stop it.

They had planned for a significant but recoverable disruption.

What they got was something else entirely.

Indianapolis lost power first. Most of the city was asleep.

The cascade moved east and south simultaneously. Columbus. Dayton. The smaller cities and towns between them going dark in sequence. Cincinnati. Two million people. The cascade still moving when the sun came up, still finding connections to take down, still spreading through a system that had no mechanism to stop it because stopping it required the backup infrastructure that had been ordered and had not arrived.

By early morning a significant portion of the American Midwest had gone dark.

In the cities, people were waking up.

They woke to alarm clocks that had not gone off. To quiet houses. To the absence of the small persistent lights that modern households accumulate without noticing. They reached for their phones. In the first hour the phones still worked, the cellular network straining but holding, long enough for people to confirm that yes, the power was out, and yes, it appeared widespread, and no, the utility company did not have a restoration estimate available.

That last part was unusual.

But it was early. People with gas stoves made coffee. People without them did without. They told themselves the power would be back soon because that was what power always did.

Forty minutes northwest of Cincinnati, in a town of 597 people, the morning was beginning the same way.

***

She changed her damp clothes in the dark by feel and went downstairs with Rufus beside her and did not bother with light switches because there was no point in light switches. The refrigerator had stopped at some point while she slept. She could tell by the quality of the silence. A house with everything running makes a particular layered sound that becomes invisible through familiarity, the way a river sounds to the people who live near it, which is to say it stops sounding like anything at all and becomes simply the texture of existing in that place. What she was standing in now was the absence of that texture. The house was more silent than silence. It was the silence of something that had been running and had stopped.

She went to the kitchen first.

Every container she could find. Every pot. Every pitcher. The large stockpot her mother had used for canning that lived in the cabinet above the refrigerator and that Emma had not touched in the two years since she moved back, lifting it down now with both hands and setting it in the sink. She filled them all from the tap while the tap still ran on municipal pressure, working methodically and without hurrying because hurrying would not change the physics of what she was doing and she needed to think clearly.

Rufus sat in the kitchen doorway and watched her work.

When the pots were full she went upstairs and filled both bathtubs. The water came out warm and then lukewarm and then cold as the water heater lost its temperature without power to maintain it. She filled them anyway. Cold water was still water.

When she came back downstairs she clipped his leash.

***

She went to the front window first.

Carnegie Hall's bell tower stood against the pre-dawn sky without its lights. The floodlights that illuminated it every night of every year that Emma could remember, that she had looked at from this window as a child and as a teenager and as the grown woman who had come back to this house to figure out what her mother had been protecting, gone. Main Street was dark in every direction. No streetlights casting their familiar orange pools on the pavement. No porch lights. No glow from a single window in either direction as far as she could see.

The town was dark the way it had been dark before anyone thought to run wires through it.

Emma stood at the window with Rufus pressed against her leg and the Irish Bowl still smoldering somewhere in the back of her mind and listened to the street. A dog barking three blocks over. The creek behind the properties on the south side of Oak Street, audible in a way it was not audible on normal nights. She had not been able to hear that creek since she moved back. The background noise of powered civilization had covered it.

She opened the front door and they went out.

***

Mr. Patterson from next door was on his porch with a coffee cup.

He was in his mid-seventies and had lived in Moores Hill his entire life and had sat on this porch through every power outage Dearborn County had produced in seven decades and he sat now with the comfortable patience of a man who has outlasted every temporary inconvenience the world has thrown at him and fully expects to outlast this one too. His coffee was in a thermos mug, the kind that keeps things hot without power. He had been using that thermos mug since before Emma was born.

"Morning Emma." He raised the cup toward her in a small salute. "Any word on when they'll have it back?"

Emma looked at him. At the thermos cup and the porch chair and the comfortable patience that decades of morning routines had given him. Mr. Patterson had outlasted everything Dearborn County had thrown at him because everything Dearborn County had thrown at him had eventually resolved.

"Not yet," she said. "Should know more later."

She kept walking.

The pre-dawn was warm already with the particular warmth of a June night that never fully cooled, the heat of the previous day still rising from the pavement. Rufus moved beside her with his nose working steadily, reading the street the way he read everything, methodically and completely and without skipping anything. Emma walked and observed.

The Hendersons had their front door open despite the early hour. Voices inside, low and urgent. She could see the thin beam of a flashlight moving across the ceiling of the front room, someone moving through the house with purpose. Their teenage son was sitting on the front steps in his pajamas looking at his phone with the particular frustrated expression of someone who keeps expecting a signal that keeps not arriving.

She gave him a small nod as she passed. He nodded back. Didn't ask her anything.

Three houses further the Kowalski place sat dark and sealed. Every window shut despite the warmth. Curtains drawn. The particular closed quality of a household that has decided the right response to uncertainty is to put as much barrier as possible between itself and whatever is happening outside.

Carol Briggs was in her driveway in a bathrobe, standing very still, looking up at the sky the way people look up at the sky when they are not actually looking at anything. Emma recognized the expression. It was the expression of someone whose internal framework for how the world works had just developed a crack and who had not yet decided how large the crack was.

"Carol," Emma said.

Carol looked at her. "The phones aren't working," she said. It came out as a simple statement of fact but underneath it was a question that was much larger than phones.

"I know," Emma said. "Come to Carnegie Hall this morning. James will have information."

Carol nodded slowly. Still looking at the sky.

Emma kept moving.

At the corner of Oak and Main she stopped.

The loose gathering she had expected was already forming on the south end of the block, not quite a crowd yet, more like the early stage of one. Eight people she recognized standing in the predawn dark with their coffee and their phones held up at angles that suggested they were still searching for signal. The faces she could read in the low light carried the expression she had been cataloguing since she left her porch. Mild inconvenience. Inconvenience with an undertone of something they were not quite naming yet. The specific human cognitive state of people who know something is wrong but have not yet built the framework for how wrong.

Not yet. She could work with not yet.

"Carnegie Hall this morning," she said as she passed. "James will have information."

A few of them nodded. One woman she didn't recognize asked if the phones were going to come back. Emma said she would know more later and kept walking.

***

Tom Hargrove had the hardware store open.

This did not surprise her. Tom was seventy-one years old and had been opening the hardware store before dawn every weekday for four decades and a power outage was not going to change his relationship with the hours of the day. The door was propped with a piece of scrap lumber and a handwritten sign was taped to the glass at eye level, the letters large and deliberate in black marker.

CASH ONLY. HONOR SYSTEM. WE KNOW WHO YOU ARE.

Emma pushed through the door. Rufus's nails on the old wood floor. The smell of the store, metal and oil and the particular smell of a building that has been selling the same categories of useful things for so long that the smell has become part of the structure itself.

Tom was behind the counter with a composition notebook open and a pen in his hand, writing down each transaction by hand with the methodical care of a man who kept good records as a matter of character rather than policy. He was telling a woman Emma recognized as Carol Park that he figured the power would be back by afternoon.

Emma let it stand.

Near the entrance, two men stood looking at the shelves with a quality of attention that was not shopping.

They were in their thirties. County road mud on their boots, the specific red-clay color of mud from the roads west of town where the soil composition was different from what surrounded Moores Hill itself. Their eyes moved across Tom's shelves with a systematic quality. Not browsing. Not looking for a specific item. They were noting what was there. Quantities. Categories. They were doing inventory.

Emma watched them for the four seconds it took to register what she was seeing and then looked away.

Tom caught her eye across the store through a gap between two customers. She held his gaze for a moment. Not the reassuring nod she had given everyone else on Main Street this morning. A different one, smaller and more specific, the nod of someone who is confirming that she has seen what he has seen. Tom held her gaze a beat longer than he needed to and then looked back at the customer in front of him and kept writing in his notebook.

Emma went to Carnegie Hall.

***

The building was unlocked as it always was.

She pushed through the heavy front door into the cool interior. Even without power, even in the pre-dawn dark, Carnegie Hall was cooler than the street outside. The building's 1907 construction held temperature through mass and thickness, the simple physics of stone and mortar that was laid before anyone had decided that machinery could do the work instead.

She went downstairs.

The basement security office ran on its own battery backup, which James had upgraded in the months following the Safety Coalition situation. The lights were on down here, dim but steady, and James was at the desk with Reeves beside him working a shortwave radio and a large paper map of the regional grid spread across the surface between them.

Both of them looked up when she came in. Rufus sat down immediately beside her left knee.

James looked settled. The particular quality of a man who has been through enough difficulty to know what the first hours require of him and has already committed to providing it.

"How far does it go?" Emma said.

"As far as we can tell," James said. "We're still trying to get a picture of the edges."

Reeves was working the shortwave with small precise adjustments, pulling fragments from across the region. Indianapolis, distorted and cutting in and out. A Cincinnati station running on emergency generator, clear and urgent, and then cut off mid-sentence and did not come back. A voice from somewhere in Ohio saying the words coordinated attack before the signal dropped and went to hiss.

Emma looked at the map.

James had been marking it by hand as the shortwave fragments confirmed what he was seeing. The marks covered most of the visible map. Indianapolis and its suburbs. Columbus. Dayton. The smaller cities and towns along the connecting corridors. The cascade moving through every interconnection point where the new infrastructure met the old without the buffer that should have been there.

She looked at where the marks stopped.

They did not stop at any visible edge of the map.

"There are no edges," Emma said.

The room was quiet for a moment

James looked at the map. Then at her. Then back at the map with the expression of a man who has been thinking exactly that and is not glad to hear it said aloud.

"No," he said. "Not that we can find."

Reeves pulled his headphones off. "Indianapolis is saying weeks. Maybe longer. They're not committing to a number but they're not saying days. The language has changed in the last hour the way it changes when the people talking have stopped believing what they were saying before."

Emma knew that quality. The particular shift in how officials spoke when they crossed from managing public concern to confronting what they actually knew.

"The town meeting needs to be this morning," she said.

"Noon," James said. "I was going to ask you to help get word out before eight."

"I'll take Main Street and you take the residential blocks."

James nodded. Already writing a list.

Emma looked at the map one more time. At Cincinnati, forty minutes to the southeast. Two million people waking up to the same dark morning. The mathematics of two million people losing power and refrigeration and communication simultaneously, the stores emptying in hours, the gas stations inaccessible, the directional pressure of a large urban population that had realized it needed to go somewhere that had what it no longer had.

She thought about the two men in Tom's hardware store. The county road mud on their boots. The systematic way their eyes had moved across the shelves.

"James," she said.

"I know," James said, without looking up from his list.

She believed him.

***

The town meeting began filling at eleven-thirty.

Not because James had asked people to come early. Because Moores Hill is a small town that knows when something is happening at its center and moves toward it without being told. They came through the Carnegie Hall doors in twos and threes and family groups and they filled the main hall the way water fills a vessel, finding the available space and settling into it. Folding chairs that Margaret Hendricks had organized that morning with the efficient calm of a woman who has been helping this building serve the community for thirty years. The overflow standing along the walls with their arms crossed or their hands in their pockets, the particular body language of people waiting for something they are not sure they want to hear.

By noon the hall held close to two hundred people.

James stood at the front without notes.

He told them what he knew without softening it. Regional grid failure across a significant portion of the Midwest. A coordinated attack on American infrastructure, sophisticated and deliberate, targeting specific vulnerabilities in the electrical system. Communication with the outside world limited and continuing to degrade as backup systems exhausted themselves. No restoration timeline from any official source he had been able to reach. The county emergency management office was aware and coordinating at the county level but Moores Hill should plan to function with significant autonomy for a period that could not yet be defined.

He stopped there and let the silence hold.

Emma stood at the side of the room and watched the faces.

The moment when information that doesn't fit the existing framework lands in a room full of people, and each person has to decide individually what to do with it. Some people processed fast and their faces showed it, the visible recalibration happening in real time. Some people went still in the specific way of someone who has received more than they can immediately integrate and has paused all non-essential functions while they work on it.

Tom Hargrove was in the second row doing arithmetic. Emma could see it. Store inventory against likely duration against the number of mouths in Moores Hill and the surrounding farms.

Mayor Patricia Ashcraft sat in the front row with a legal pad on her knee and a pen in her hand, writing steadily. Patricia processed fastest of anyone in the room.

"How long are we talking?" Tom Hargrove asked.

His voice was level. He needed the number for the arithmetic he was doing and was not afraid of it.

"We don't know," James said. Without apology. "Which is why we plan today as if it is going to be a long time. Planning for short and being wrong costs us everything. Planning for long and being wrong costs us nothing."

A woman near the back raised her hand. "My mother is in Cincinnati. She lives alone. Is there any way to—"

"The mail is still operating," James said. "Limited and slower than normal but operating. Write to her today. Gerald Sims at the post office can tell you what's available."

Earl Hendricks said without raising his hand: "We've got cattle to feed and a generator that runs on diesel and about three weeks of diesel on the property. What happens after three weeks?"

"That's the conversation I want to have with you and the other farm families this afternoon," James said. "Right after this. Carnegie Hall basement. What you have and what you need and what the community can contribute in both directions."

More questions came and James answered them all with the same level directness. Not reassuring people falsely. Not pretending the picture was different from what it was. Giving the room the thing a community under pressure needs more than reassurance, which is the clear sense that the person at the front is looking at the actual situation and is going to keep looking at it honestly regardless of what it shows.

When the questions slowed he told them what the next twenty-four hours would look like. The farm meeting this afternoon. A community resource inventory starting tomorrow morning. The mail situation and what Gerald Sims needed from volunteers. The daily briefing at Carnegie Hall at six PM for as long as it was useful.

"One more thing," James said.

The room went quiet.

"Moores Hill has been through hard things before. This is a hard thing. What I know about this town, after growing up in it and spending twelve years as its deputy, is that hard things bring out something in communities that ordinary times don't. I'm not interested in speeches about it. I'm just telling you what I've seen. What you do in the next few days will determine what the next few months look like. I think you're going to do it right."

He stopped.

Patricia Ashcraft closed her legal pad.

The room began to move.

***

Robert Caldwell came to his desk at his normal hour and found his monitoring systems already dark.

He sat down with his coffee, black, the same as he had taken it for twenty-three years in Peru, and opened his access points one by one with the methodical patience of a man who has performed this ritual every morning for twenty years and knows exactly what healthy looks like.

He found nothing.

Not slow connections. Not degraded performance. Nothing. Each access point returning the same complete absence, the servers simply not there, the connections that had taken him twenty years of careful work to build going silent without announcement.

He sat with that.

Outside his window the Peruvian night was going about its business as it always did. The sounds of the community around him. Animals. The distant sound of the Valdez household beginning its morning. He missed Linda. He missed her in the mornings specifically, in the way that absence makes itself felt most clearly at the times when presence used to be most ordinary. She had been a morning person in the particular Indiana way, up before him, moving through the kitchen with the comfortable efficiency of someone in their own space. He had been trying to get used to that absence for twenty-three years and had not entirely gotten used to it.

He worked backward through his cached data. The timestamps told him the cascade had moved through the American Midwest while he slept. Indianapolis first. Then east and south. Then the corridors between the cities. Then everything.

Everything he had spent fifteen years building toward. The monitoring infrastructure, the database access, the window into American records systems that let him watch the seven sites and the families and the patterns that suggested what was coming. All of it dependent on servers that were now dark.

He was blind in the specific way that was worse than ordinary blindness. He could see perfectly. He simply could not see the things he needed to see.

Then he found the fragment.

Cached in his system in the final seconds before the missing persons database connection dropped. A partial result from a search that was not his search. Someone else had been running his query. The same coordinates he ran every week. The same essential question, asked through a slightly different methodology but unmistakably the same inquiry, pointing unmistakably at the same thing.

Someone had been looking for him.

Someone had found the ghost pattern.

Robert Caldwell set his coffee down and looked at the fragment with the full quality of his attention, which was considerable and which had been expanded by twenty-three years of ceremonial work into something that most people who encountered it found somewhat unsettling. He turned it over. He examined it from every angle. He did not treat it as coincidence because he had learned over two decades that the details that felt like coincidence were never coincidence.

This was not a government search. He knew what government searches looked like in database architecture and this was not that. This was a single person or a very small team, working carefully and with genuine understanding of what they were looking for.

He thought about the Moores Hill site.

He thought about Linda, who had spent thirty plus years protecting something she did not fully understand, sustained by the instinct that it needed protecting.

He thought about Emma, who had been eight years old when he left and was now a grown woman, living in Moores Hill, the heir to the Moore bloodline whether she knew it or not.

He sat in the dark of his own making, surrounded by the Peruvian pre-dawn, and turned that thought over very carefully.

Someone knew he existed.

He did not yet know who.

But he was beginning to form a suspicion that sat in his chest with the particular weight of something that was going to require him to make a decision he had been postponing for a very long time.

He picked up his pen and began to write.

CHAPTER 2: THE FIRST 48

James had been through emergencies before.

Two tours overseas had taught him things about human behavior under pressure that no civilian training program adequately covered. Not the dramatic things. The quiet things. The way a person's voice changed in the second hour of a crisis versus the first. The way a group of strangers would, under the right conditions and the wrong circumstances, become something that functioned like a unit. The way the decisions made in the first hours shaped everything that came after them, not because the decisions were always correct but because they established the pattern, and pattern under pressure becomes structure, and structure is what keeps people alive when the situation does not improve.

Growing up in Dearborn County had added to it. More granular. More personal. He knew the names of the people in this county and the names of their children and the particular ways that different families responded when something went wrong. He knew which households would dig in and help their neighbors and which would lock their doors and wait for someone else to solve it. He knew who the veterans were and what branch and roughly what they had done. He knew the farms and the roads and the particular geography of Dearborn County in the way that a man knows ground he has driven every day for most of his life, which is to say he knew it in his body rather than just his mind.

All of that was available to him now.

***

He left Carnegie Hall at one in the afternoon with a list in his shirt pocket. Twelve names. Farmers first, then veterans, then two conversations he needed to have with specific people before the end of the day.

He took the truck north toward Earl Hendricks's farm.

Earl was in the equipment shed when James pulled in. Not hiding from the situation. Working through it. He heard the truck and came to the shed door, wiping his hands on a cloth that had been wiping hands for decades by the look of it. Seventy-three years old and built like a man who had been doing physical work every day of those seventy-three years and intended to keep doing it.

"Figured you'd come out today," Earl said.

"Wanted to talk before tonight's meeting," James said.

Earl leaned against the shed doorframe. "Tell me what you actually think. Not what you said in that room."

James told him. The same assessment he had given the town meeting but without the careful pacing, without the management of how information lands in a large group of people with different capacities for difficult news. Earl Hendricks had been farming through drought years and flood years and years when the market did what it occasionally did to the people who depended on it. He deserved the unmanaged version.

Earl listened without interrupting. When James finished he was quiet for a moment, looking at the fields.

"Cattle are going to be the problem," he said. "Feed costs money and I can't run my fuel indefinitely. But the pasture is good right now. I can run them on grass through the summer if I have to. Winter is the question."

"Winter is five months away," James said.

"Winter is always five months away until it isn't," Earl said. He looked at James. "What do you need from me right now?"

"The perimeter conversation tonight. And your read on which of the other farm families are solid."

"Kowalski and Miller without question. The Briggs family." Earl thought for a moment. "Dale Ford on the south road has been having a hard year but he's steady under pressure. I'd include him."

James wrote the names in his notebook.

***

He worked through the afternoon that way. Farm to farm. Each conversation different because each family was different. The Miller farm. The Kowalski place. Dale Briggs, who listened with the particular tight-jawed attention of a man already calculating his diesel supply against the number of months James was not quite saying. Dale Ford on the south road, who asked the right questions in the right order and said yes before James finished explaining.

By four in the afternoon he had what he needed from the farm families. By four-thirty he had spoken to seven of the twelve veterans on his list. Not all of them said yes. Roy Simmons was sixty-eight years old with a bad knee and three grandchildren living with him since his daughter's situation had changed in the spring, and Roy said he wanted to help but James needed to understand his situation. James understood his situation. He crossed Roy's name off the list and wrote it at the bottom of a different one.

By the time he pulled back onto Main Street it was getting toward five and the block party was in full production.

***

He had not planned the block party. Nobody had planned it. It had simply emerged from the particular human instinct that kicks in when people are confronted with something they cannot immediately solve and find that the most available response is to feed each other.

It had started on Elm Street the previous evening, someone pulling their grill to the curb and cooking everything in their freezer before it spoiled, their neighbors doing the same. By the morning of Day 2 it had moved to Main Street itself. Grills and camp stoves lined up along the sidewalk, folding tables covered with everything perishable that the households of Moores Hill had been carrying in their refrigerators and freezers since the grid went down. Come eat. It's all going bad anyway. Come eat.

James parked at the end of the block and stood at the corner of Main and Oak and watched.

The children were the clearest sign. Moores Hill's children had been released from the particular captivity of screens and schedules and were running through yards and streets with the loose exhilarated energy of kids who had been handed an unexpected holiday and were not yet old enough to understand why it had arrived. Older kids sat on curbs in groups, talking to each other in the way they rarely talked when their phones were working, which was with their faces turned toward the person they were talking to.

Their parents stood on porches and sidewalks talking to neighbors they had not spoken to properly in months. Gerald Park was on his front porch having what appeared to be a real conversation with the young couple who had moved in next door eighteen months ago. James had never seen them talk. They were talking now, all three of them leaning slightly toward each other the way people lean when they are genuinely interested in what the other person is saying, Gerald with a plate of food in his hand and the young husband with a baby on his hip and his wife laughing at something Gerald had just said.

James watched and let himself feel the particular complicated thing that the block party was producing in him.

It was good. Genuinely good. He was not going to take that from Moores Hill because he had done arithmetic.

He was also watching the freezers emptying onto the folding tables and doing the arithmetic anyway. Everything on those tables was food that had been in the supply chain before the grid went down and was not going to be replaced. Every steak and chicken breast and bag of frozen corn that went onto a paper plate was food that was not going to be there in three weeks.

The stores were not restocking. The trucks were not coming. What Moores Hill had was what it had.

James let the block party run.

He walked through it and accepted a plate from his sister Sarah McClanahan, who had set up at a table near the diner and was running an informal feeding station with the efficiency of someone who had been feeding large numbers of people in compressed timeframes her entire professional life. She handed him a plate with the particular look she gave people when she knew they had been moving all day and probably hadn't eaten.

"Sit down for five minutes," she said.

"I've got more stops to make," James said.

"Five minutes," Sarah said. "You're no good to anyone if you fall over."

He sat on the curb and ate and watched Main Street and thought about what needed to happen before the end of the day.

***

He found Tom Hargrove at the back of the hardware store at six, after Tom had locked the front door and turned the CLOSED sign in the window.

"I was wondering when you'd come," Tom said.

"I need you to stop selling," James said. "Not publicly. Just start turning the sales down. You're sick of the lines. You're doing a deep inventory. Whatever reason makes sense. But I need to know what you have."

Tom walked James through the shelves in the back room, pulling items and naming quantities in a low voice. The composition notebook came out. Tom had already started writing it down.

They spent forty minutes in the back room going through what was there.

When they were done Tom looked at his list and then at James. "You're thinking months," he said.

"I'm planning for months," James said.

Tom nodded slowly. The distinction mattered to him and he showed that it mattered. "I'll manage what I've got. You let me know what the community needs and I'll be straight with you about whether I can cover it."

James shook his hand and went next to Dale Mercer at the grocery.

***

Dale had locked the grocery store on the morning of Day 2, overwhelmed by the buying of the first day and uncertain about what came next. He was in the back office when James knocked on the delivery entrance, sitting at his desk in the particular posture of a man who has been not knowing what to do for several hours and is running low on the energy required to keep not knowing.

He looked relieved when James came through the door.

They went through it the same way he had gone through it with Tom. What was in the store. What the daily consumption of Moores Hill looked like under normal conditions. What different scenarios of duration meant for how long the inventory would last.

Dale had the numbers in his head. He walked James through the back storage and the walk-in cooler, which was warming toward the temperature of the storage room around it.

"The perishables are mostly gone," Dale said. "Dairy, meat. Most of it went in the first day and a half."

"What keeps?" James said.

"Long term? Canned goods, dry beans, rice, flour. Pasta. Reasonable quantities." He paused. "Not unlimited."

"How long?" James said.

Dale looked at the storage room around them, doing the same math that Tom Hargrove had been doing all day. "At normal Moores Hill consumption levels, if nobody comes in from outside? A few months. Maybe a little more." He looked at James. "But if word gets around that we've got food."

"I know," James said.

"That's not months," Dale said.

"Keep the store closed for now. I'll tell you when to open it and on what terms. What I need from you tonight is an inventory. Everything you have, everything it would take to run a controlled distribution."

Dale was quiet for a moment. He was a man who had run a business his whole adult life on the principle of selling things to people who came in to buy them. The idea of controlled distribution sat sideways against everything he had built.

But he was also a man who understood arithmetic.

"Okay," he said. "I'll have it ready by tomorrow morning."

***

The math landed on Day 3.

Not for everyone at once. It moved through Moores Hill the way significant realizations move through small communities, person by person, conversation by conversation. James watched it happen from the Carnegie Hall basement, people coming to him with questions and him answering them as honestly as the situation allowed.

How long will this last? We don't know. Plan for a long time.

Is help coming? The county knows. We can't confirm timelines.

What should I do with the food I have left? Be careful with it. What you have is what you have now.

That last answer was the one that changed faces. James watched people receive it and do the calculation behind their eyes and arrive at the specific regret of someone who had put their entire freezer on a folding table two days ago and now understood with complete and irreversible clarity that it was not going to be replaced.

He did not say anything to make that feeling smaller. There was nothing honest he could say. What he could do was make sure the regret produced action rather than paralysis. He told each person who came to him the same three things. Come to the six o'clock briefing. Bring whatever food you have that keeps. Tell your neighbors.

By the time Reeves and Emma arrived at seven, James had a hand-drawn map on the table, drafted on Tom Hargrove's donated paper. Every farm. Every road. Every natural approach to Moores Hill from the south and east where the county highways connected back toward Cincinnati.

Emma looked at it when she came in and was quiet for a moment.

"The Hendricks farm is the northern anchor," she said.

"Yes," James said.

"And if something comes from the east?"

James pointed to the Miller farm. "Miller is here. His land runs along the county road for about a mile before it turns. You can't get to the eastern approach without passing his fence line."

Reeves set a sheet of paper on the table. His own accounting. The shortwave radio, fully operational. Generator fuel in the Carnegie Hall basement, measured that afternoon. The county emergency management channel, intermittent but functioning. Three other licensed shortwave operators in Moores Hill, two with solar capability, one who had asked Reeves directly that morning to keep his name out of any public communications about it. James had filed it and would honor it. Resources attracted attention.

"The farms can sustain protein and produce through the summer growing season," James said. "Dale's inventory covers dry goods and canned goods for several months at controlled consumption. Tom's situation is tighter. The constraint is going to be controlled consumption holding against what comes from outside."

"What comes from outside," Emma said.

"Pressure," James said. He looked at the map. At the roads leading south and east toward Cincinnati. "The two men Tom had in the hardware store yesterday morning, those weren't the first. Reeves had two different reports from the county roads the day before. Vehicles moving slowly. Not lost. Looking."

Emma was quiet. She had told him about the two men and he had noted it and not said anything in the town meeting and she had understood why.

"How long before it becomes organized?" she said.

"Less time than we would like," James said.

Reeves looked at the map. "We need eyes on the roads."

"Starting tomorrow. The farm families are in. Eleven veterans committed. Reeves, you said two officers on rotation."

"Two on, two off. It's what I've got."

James nodded. He looked at the numbers across the desk and the map and felt the weight of a man who has done the assessment honestly and knows that honest assessment is not the same as comfortable assessment. The margin was thin. Not catastrophic, not yet, not if the community held together and managed what it had and the farm families could produce through the summer. But thin margins had a way of becoming thinner under pressure, and the pressure was coming from forty minutes to the southeast where two million people were waking up every morning to a situation that was not improving.

"One more thing," Emma said.

James looked at her.

"The two strangers from the hardware store didn't come back today."

"No," James said.

"That's not because they gave up," Emma said.

"No," James said. "It's because they went back to report what they found."

The three of them looked at the map.

Outside Carnegie Hall, Moores Hill was settling into its third night without power. The fireflies were moving across the dark lawn, unchallenged by any competing light, extraordinary in a way that James had not noticed in years. He could see them through the narrow basement window near the ceiling, the small cold fires of them moving through the dark with a patience that had nothing to do with what human beings were doing or planning or worrying about.

He turned back to the map.

There was always more work to do.

CHAPTER 3: PAPER AND MEMORY

Carnegie Hall was cooler than the rest of Moores Hill.

Emma had known this in the abstract, the way you know things about buildings you have been in and out of your whole life without consciously registering them. But on the fourth day of the outage, when the June heat had settled into the town with the particular persistence of summer warmth that has no air conditioning to push back against it, the difference became something she felt the moment she pushed through the front door. The building's 1907 construction held temperature through mass and thickness, the simple physics of stone and mortar laid by men who understood the building would be standing long after they were not.

People had started coming without being invited.

Not for the operations center in the basement, though that was drawing its own steady traffic. People were coming to the main hall itself. Families with children. Elderly residents from the blocks nearest Main Street. The building's construction had always known what it had never needed to advertise. Solid walls and high ceilings do in summer what electricity used to do.

Emma arrived at eight in the morning and found eleven people already settled in. By noon there were closer to thirty, Margaret Hendricks had appeared at some point with a folding table and a coffee urn running on a camp stove and a handwritten sign that read COMMUNITY INFORMATION. People gravitated to it the way people gravitate to any source of certainty in uncertain times.

Emma set up at a table near the east windows.

She had her custodian notebook. Robert Moore's journal. A set of physical files assembled over the past three months from the historical society's public records collection, brought home one folder at a time with the deliberate patience of someone who understood that good investigative work was built from primary sources regardless of what digital tools were also available. And

Rufus, who settled under the table with the focused patience of a dog who had learned that his person's work required stillness.

She opened the notebook and looked at what she had.

Three months of careful work. The custodian network she had been building through encrypted channels. The father thread she had been following through database cross-referencing and records searches. All of it dependent on infrastructure that had stopped functioning four days ago.

She sat with the full weight of that for a moment and let herself feel it completely. Then she picked up her pen.

***

The two letters had been drafted and redrafted for weeks.

Not because she didn't know what to say. The hesitation had been about timing, about the irreversibility of sending them, about the recognition that putting words on paper and mailing them to addresses on other continents was a different kind of commitment than sending an encrypted message that could be amended within minutes if the wording was wrong. Paper moved slowly. Paper arrived with the full weight of whatever had been written on it, unable to be softened by a follow-up sent ten minutes later.

The grid failure had resolved her hesitation the way certain kinds of pressure resolve things. When the careful path closes, the direct path opens. She had the wording. She had the addresses, verified through three separate sources before the power went down and written in her notebook precisely because she had understood that a backup for every digital record was not paranoia but practice.

She wrote the final versions at the Carnegie Hall table while thirty Moores Hill residents moved quietly through the building around her.

One letter to the family in England. One to Peru.

She addressed both envelopes carefully and put them in her bag. Then she found James in the basement.

"I need to get to Lawrenceburg," she said.

He looked up from the community resource map. "Gas situation is manageable for now. Stay on the main roads. There have been more strangers on the county roads since yesterday."

"I'll be two hours," she said.

***

The drive to Lawrenceburg was twenty minutes on a normal day. On Day 4 it was a different drive on the same road.

Three cars in twenty minutes where she would normally have counted thirty or more. A man on a bicycle on the shoulder, saddlebags loaded, moving toward Lawrenceburg. Two people walking along the road past the Miller farm turnoff, carrying backpacks, moving away from Moores Hill. Emma watched them in her rearview mirror and thought about where they had come from and where they were going and what they expected to find.

Without the hum of highway traffic, without the distant industrial undertone of the region's normal operations, she could hear the fields. The wind in the corn. A tractor somewhere to the north doing the work the season required. She had grown up close enough to this that something in her recognized it. Not nostalgia. Recognition. The land doing what it always did.

***

The Lawrenceburg post office was open.

She had expected a locked door and a handwritten closure notice. Instead the door was propped and the branch manager, Carol Deitz, was behind the counter fielding difficult questions with the composure of someone who had found, through the process of fielding them, a way to be genuinely useful despite having very few complete answers.

What stopped Emma when she walked in was the walls. Every available surface covered in bulletins. Handwritten notices in careful block letters. Printed sheets from one of the last printer runs before the power went down. She stood in the doorway and read the nearest one.

The postal service had reorganized itself.

No business mail. No advertising. Personal and emergency correspondence only. A waiver system for citizens who could not afford postage. And a provision Emma read twice: no home delivery. Citizens were responsible for bringing mail to their local post office for both sending and receiving.

"When did this come through?" she asked Carol.

"Day two," Carol said. "A driver came from Indianapolis with a vehicle full of these and about four hours of information about how we were expected to operate going forward. Haven't seen a truck since. Mail is accumulating."

Emma looked at the outgoing bin behind the counter. Dozens of envelopes stacked and sorted and going nowhere.

"What does move the mail right now?" Emma asked.

"Nothing centrally. Once a community can organize its own run to the next distribution point it starts moving again. That's on each community to figure out."

Emma set her two envelopes on the counter.

"International," she said.

Carol looked at the addresses. "Once they reach a distribution center with outbound capacity they'll move. International systems are functioning. It's the domestic leg that's the problem." She took the envelopes with the particular care of someone who understood that each one represented something a person needed to send. "I'll do my best."

Emma believed her. She took the information packet and drove back toward Moores Hill.

***

She stopped at the Moores Hill post office on the north end of Main Street before she went anywhere else.

Gerald Sims had been the postmaster for eleven years. He was a methodical man with the patient reliability that small town postal operations required. He was sitting behind the counter in the dark with a battery lantern and the expression of a man who has been waiting for someone to tell him what to do and has been too conscientious about his role to do anything until someone does.

Emma put the information packet on the counter in front of him.

He read it slowly. Twice. She watched him work through it, the resistance of a system encountering input that requires it to reconfigure, then the processing, then the settling into the new shape.

"What does this mean for us?" Gerald asked.

She walked him through it. The mail run, Moores Hill volunteers driving to Lawrenceburg on whatever schedule the community's fuel situation supported. Outgoing mail accumulating here and going out on the run. Incoming coming back the same way. The end of home delivery.

"I can manage the sorting and the counter," he said. "I need the community to handle the run."

"Tonight's meeting," Emma said. "I'll put it on the agenda."

***

Dorothy Webb was at her desk with a battery lamp.

Dorothy had worked at the Moores Hill Historical Society for twenty-six years and had developed over that time the particular relationship with primary sources that long archival work produces, the ability to sit with documents for hours without losing focus, the patience to follow a thread through materials that were not organized around the question being asked. Emma had come to respect that quality in her. They had developed a working rhythm over three months of research visits.

"Back again," Dorothy said.

"Back again," Emma confirmed.

She found her table near the south window and settled Rufus under it and opened the boxes she had been working through for the past two weeks.

The county estate records from 2000 through 2005. Specifically the Caldwell estate, filed and processed through the county in early 2002 following the reported death of Robert Caldwell in a single-vehicle accident on the interstate outside Columbus.

Emma had learned, through years of work in data security, that the most significant information in any dataset was often defined by its absence. A system running correctly produced certain kinds of output in certain patterns. Deviations from those patterns were where the real information lived. She applied the same discipline to the estate records.

Real estate proceedings had texture. The messiness of human lives being sorted through by a process designed not for elegance but for thoroughness. Amendments. Corrections. Small administrative correspondence between multiple parties. Forms filed on the wrong date and refiled correctly. Signatures obtained out of sequence and the record corrected with marginal notations. The specific messiness of real human processes conducted by real human beings who made small errors and corrected them as they went.

The Caldwell estate record did not have that texture.

It was complete. Internally consistent. Every form filed on schedule. Every signature in the correct sequence. Every piece of supporting documentation present and properly organized. She went through it three times looking for the normal messiness of a real estate proceeding and found instead the particular cleanliness of something that had been constructed rather than assembled.

She wrote that observation in her notebook in the shorthand she used for things she was not yet ready to name directly.

Then she went looking for what should be there and was not.

Three things were missing from the Caldwell estate that should have been present in any estate of this size and complexity. She wrote them in her notebook. One, two, three. Each one a gap where documentation should exist and did not.

For a legitimate estate proceeding to be complete without them, someone with significant legal and financial authority would have had to make specific decisions about how the estate was structured and documented. Not carelessly. Deliberately. The absence was not sloppy. It was the absence that resulted from someone who knew exactly what they were doing deciding that these three things would not be part of the official record.

She wrote a name in her notebook. Not Robert Caldwell's name. The name of the person whose authority and access would have been required to produce a record that was complete without those three things.

She underlined it twice.

Then she found the estate filing and confirmed what she needed. The executor of record. The attorney who had filed the estate and managed its processing through the county system. A man named Franklin Marsh. A Cincinnati address on Montgomery Road listed as his office of practice.

She wrote his name in her notebook under the first name. Underlined it once.

Two names. One estate. One deliberate set of absences.

The light through the south windows had moved significantly while she worked. Early afternoon. Rufus stirred under the table, shifted his position, settled again. Dorothy was reading at her desk with the composed patience of a woman who had been reading in this building for twenty-six years and was not going to stop because the phones were down.

Emma drafted the letter to Franklin Marsh at the archive table. Professional and brief. She identified herself as a researcher with questions regarding the administration of the Caldwell estate and asked if Mr. Marsh would be willing to speak with her at his convenience. She gave Carnegie Hall as a return address. She acknowledged that postal delivery was operating under emergency conditions and asked him to respond as quickly as circumstances allowed.

She did not tell him what she was looking for.

A good investigator did not show the hand before the conversation began.

She folded the letter and addressed the envelope and put it in her bag.

***

Gerald Sims had spent the afternoon implementing. He had reorganized the counter operation, set up a clear incoming and outgoing system, and made a handwritten sign for the window that explained the new situation in direct language. Emma read it through the glass and found it accurate and complete. Gerald had understood the assignment.

She added her envelope to his outgoing stack. He noted each one in his ledger.

"Going out on tomorrow's run," he said.

"Thank you Gerald," Emma said.

She drove home in the early evening with Rufus beside her and the custodian notebook open on the passenger seat. The digital tools she had spent three months building were inaccessible until the grid came back on whatever timeline the grid was going to come back on. What she had instead was paper and physical records and the ability to read them carefully and the name of a lawyer in Cincinnati who had processed a death she was becoming increasingly certain had never actually happened.

Data security had taught her that the most sophisticated intrusions were never detected through the presence of something wrong. They were detected through the absence of something right. A log entry missing where a log entry should exist. A record clean where a record should be messy.

The Caldwell estate record was the cleanest record she had ever found.

She turned onto Oak Street with Carnegie Hall's bell tower visible against the fading sky and thought about her father, whom she had believed was dead for twenty-three years, and about the name Franklin Marsh written in her notebook with a single underline, and about what a man with serious legal authority and serious knowledge of the custodian network would have needed to do to help another man disappear completely in 2002.

She went inside and fed Rufus and sat at the kitchen table with the notebook open and wrote three words at the top of a fresh page.

Find Franklin Marsh.

She looked at the words for a moment.

Then she turned the page and started planning how.

CHAPTER 4: THE FIRST WAVE

By the end of the first week James had a map.

Not a digital map. A hand-drawn one on the largest sheet of drafting paper Tom Hargrove had found in a back room and donated without being asked, a generous piece of paper that Tom had smoothed flat on the Carnegie Hall basement desk and weighted at the corners with whatever was available, a coffee mug and two evidence binders and the shortwave radio that Reeves had moved to the far end of the table to make room for it.

James had been filling it in over three days of driving the roads surrounding Moores Hill, confirming what he already knew from twelve years as a deputy and adding the details that mattered now specifically. Every farm by name and family. Every access road, paved and unpaved, the county roads and the field lanes and the two-track paths that ran between properties and showed up on no official map but that anyone who had grown up in this county or worked it long enough knew as well as the named roads. Every natural approach to Moores Hill from the directions that mattered, which were south and east where the county highways connected back toward the population centers and east where the county road ran along the edge of farmland that backed up against the kind of rural terrain that people moved through when they did not want to be seen moving.

He had pinned it to the wall of the basement and stood in front of it each morning with a cup of coffee that had been made on a camp stove and was not as good as the coffee he made at home but was hot and was there.

He stood in front of it the way he stood in front of everything that required his full attention, which was with patience and without the expectation of finding what he was looking for. Expectation narrowed vision. He had learned that early and it had served him well in two different careers. You looked at what was actually there. You did not look for the thing you had already decided was there.

What was actually there, by the morning of Day 7, was a pattern.

***

It had started on Day 5.

A report from the Henderson farm on the eastern edge of town, delivered in person by Paul Henderson at the morning briefing because there was no other way to deliver it. Tools missing from an unlocked outbuilding. A wheelbarrow. Two shovels. A hand saw. A come-along ratchet strap that Paul had been particularly specific about because he'd had it for twenty years and it had never given him a problem and he did not appreciate losing it.

Small things. The kind of things that could have been misplaced or borrowed by a neighbor who intended to return them and had not yet gotten around to it. Paul had checked with his neighbors. Nobody had borrowed anything.

James wrote it down and did not say anything about it to anyone except Reeves. One data point was not a pattern. One data point was one data point.

Day 6. The Kowalski place to the north. A barn door that Steve Kowalski had latched himself before going to bed, he was certain of it, he had done it every night of his adult life and he was not starting to forget things, standing open in the morning. Not forced. The latch had not been broken or damaged. Someone had opened it from the outside, which required knowing where the latch was and how it worked, looked inside, assessed what was there, and left without taking anything.

James noted the assessment quality of it. Not taking. Looking. Making decisions about what was there and what it was worth coming back for.

He wrote it down and said nothing beyond Reeves.

Day 7. Dale Briggs on the southeastern road woke to find his truck gone.

Not a neighbor. Not a family member. Not a misunderstanding. The truck was gone with the particular finality of something that had been taken by people who knew what they wanted and had come specifically to get it. Dale had been planning to use that truck for his portion of the community mail run to Lawrenceburg. He had told three people about that plan in the past two days. He had also used it two days earlier to drive a load of feed from his barn to the Miller farm, which meant it had been on the county road recently and could have been seen by anyone driving that road.

James sat with that last detail for a long time.

Three incidents. Seven days. He looked at his map and found the three farm locations and drew a slow line connecting them and looked at what the line suggested about direction of approach and departure.

The line pointed southeast.

Toward Cincinnati.

He put the pen down and looked at the map and felt something settle in his chest that was not quite concern and not quite certainty but the specific place between the two where his instincts lived and where he had learned, over many years, to pay attention.

This was not random.

***

He had seen this progression before.

Not here. Not in Dearborn County where the emergencies were of a different scale and character. Overseas, in the particular situations that a certain kind of military deployment produced, and in the early years of his law enforcement career when he had worked cases that other deputies had not wanted to work because they required a tolerance for ambiguity and a willingness to sit with incomplete information longer than was comfortable.

The progression from opportunistic taking to deliberate targeting had a shape that was recognizable once you had seen it enough times. The opportunistic phase was characterized by targets of convenience. Unlocked doors. Visible resources. Easy access with minimal planning. People taking what they could reach without significant investment in understanding what they were taking or from whom.

The deliberate phase looked different. It had a logic. A selection process. Targets were chosen for what they had rather than how easy they were to reach. The risk calculation shifted. People in the deliberate phase were willing to invest more effort and accept more risk to get to a specific thing they had decided they needed.

The Briggs truck was a deliberate target.

Dale Briggs was known in the community as someone who maintained his vehicles and kept his fuel tank full. That was community knowledge, the kind of thing that was simply true about a person and known to anyone who knew him. It was also exactly the kind of knowledge that someone outside the community could acquire by watching and listening and asking the right casual questions of the right people over a few days.

Someone had known the truck was there and had known it was worth taking.

James folded the map along lines he had made for exactly this purpose and put it in his shirt pocket and went to find Patricia Ashcraft.

***

The mayor's office was two blocks from Carnegie Hall.

Patricia had been keeping a presence there through the outage hours, the particular decision of a mayor who understood that part of her role was visibility, that a community in an uncertain situation needed to be able to find its elected leadership in the place where leadership was supposed to be found. She had a battery lamp on the desk and a legal pad that was accumulating notes at a rate that suggested she had not stopped thinking since the town meeting.

She looked up when James came through the door with the particular expression of someone who has been expecting a specific conversation and is ready for it.

He laid it out. The three incidents. The timeline. The progression he recognized from experience he did not fully explain but that Patricia had known him long enough to understand carried weight. He presented the facts without speculation beyond what the facts supported. One data point was one data point. Three data points with a directional pattern was something else.

She absorbed it with the stillness she brought to things that required significant internal reorganization.

"You think it's organized," she said.

"I think it's becoming organized," James said. "Right now it's still in the early phase. People from outside the area who are running short and have identified this community as having what they need. As the situation outside gets worse the approach becomes more deliberate and the people making it become more coordinated."

Patricia looked at the map he had unfolded on her desk. At the three marked locations and the line connecting them. "How much time before it becomes a serious problem?"

"Less than we would like," James said. "The block party on Day 2 was visible from the county road. Anyone who drove past and saw a community that appeared to have enough food to share it freely with neighbors is going to remember that."

Patricia was quiet. Outside her window Main Street was going about its seventh day without power with the particular adapted rhythm of a community that had stopped expecting restoration and started building routines around the reality of its absence. People moved differently than they had a week ago. Slower in some ways, more purposeful in others, the casual energy of normal daily life replaced by the focused economy of people who were managing resources consciously.

"What do you need?" she said.

"Authority to organize a community watch," James said. "I want to be precise about what I mean by that. Not a militia. Not anything that looks or functions like a military operation. A structured neighborhood watch with law enforcement coordination behind it. Reeves has officers he can contribute on rotation. I have veterans in this community with the training and the disposition for this kind of work. I need your authorization to ask them formally so they understand this is sanctioned and not something they're doing on their own initiative."

"You have it," Patricia said. "What else?"

"A communication system between the farms. We need the families on the perimeter to be able to signal toward town if something happens at their property. Without telephones that means a physical system. Agreed signals. Scheduled check-ins. A driver doing the farm circuit at regular intervals."

"Tonight's briefing," Patricia said.

"First item," James said.

Patricia looked at him steadily. "That serious?"

"The Briggs truck is gone," James said. "Yes. That serious."

***

He spent the rest of that day building.

Not announcing. Not holding meetings or making speeches or creating the kind of visible security apparatus that generated its own kind of anxiety in a community that was already managing significant stress. He moved through Moores Hill with the quiet purposefulness he brought to everything since Day 1 and had individual conversations rather than group ones, because individual conversations allowed him to calibrate what he was asking to the person he was asking it of, and because the thing he was building required people who understood specifically what they were committing to.

The veterans first.

He had been keeping a mental list of the veterans in Moores Hill for twelve years. Not formally. Not in any document. It was simply the kind of knowledge that accumulated when you worked long enough in a small enough place and paid the kind of attention that his particular background had made habitual. He knew who had served and in what branch and roughly what their experience had been. He knew which ones still carried themselves with the particular physical economy of people who had been trained to move efficiently and had never entirely stopped. He knew which ones had remained capable and which ones had let that capability go in the particular way that civilian life occasionally encouraged.

He visited each one personally. Walked up to their door or found them in their yard or their barn and stood with them and explained what he was seeing and what he was asking in direct language that did not minimize either the commitment or the purpose.

What he found surprised him, or would have surprised him if he had not learned long ago to stop being surprised by the particular way that certain people responded when a situation finally matched their preparation.

Every one of them said yes.

Not reluctantly. Not after extended negotiation about what the commitment involved and whether they could manage it around their other responsibilities. They said yes the way people say yes when they have been waiting, without knowing they were waiting, for someone to ask them to do the thing they were actually suited for.

Roy Simmons was sixty-eight with a bad knee and three grandchildren living with him and he said he couldn't do the physical work but he could run the communication relay from his house and he had a shortwave setup that James had not known about. James put him on a different list.

Gary Whitfield, who had been an Army Ranger and had been managing a hardware supply business and coaching youth baseball since he came home fourteen years ago, stood in his driveway and listened to James with his arms at his sides and his eyes doing the thing that certain people's eyes did when they were assessing a situation with the full capability of their training, and said: "Tell me what you need and when you need it."

James told him.

***

Reeves contributed two officers for rotating coverage on the main road entries. James placed them not at the entry points themselves but back from them, positioned to observe without creating a formal checkpoint that might generate confrontation before confrontation was necessary. A checkpoint announced that the community was afraid and was defending itself. A watch position simply watched. The distinction mattered in ways that were difficult to explain to people who had not managed these situations before but that James understood from experience to be significant.

The McClanahan family network became the farm communication backbone.

This was not something James engineered. It was something that already existed and that he knew better than anyone, because it was his own family's network. His and Sarah's cousins and the extended web of McClanahan connections built across three generations of Dearborn County life knew every road and property line and fence post and access point in the surrounding area in the particular way that people know ground they have worked their whole lives. Not from a map. From their feet and their hands and the accumulated memory of moving through that specific land in every season and condition over many years.

James sat with three of them at Sarah's diner on the morning of Day 7, the diner running on a propane setup that Sarah had installed two years ago for exactly no reason she could have articulated at the time beyond the sense that having a backup was better than not having one, and sketched out what he needed on a piece of paper.

Which farms to check and in what order and at what time of day and what the signal was if something was wrong.

They worked it out together, which was the right way to work it out, because the people who knew the ground knew things that no outside planner could know, which turnoffs were visible from which roads, which fence lines ran where, which properties had natural sight lines to their neighbors and which were isolated enough that a problem there could develop unobserved for hours.

They settled on something simple. A red cloth hung from a specific fence post meant trouble. A white cloth meant all clear. A daily driver would make the circuit at dawn and at dusk and report to James at Carnegie Hall.

Simple enough to remember under stress. Clear enough to act on immediately. Requiring nothing but cloth and a fence post and someone willing to make the drive twice a day.

"My cousin Earl can do the morning circuit," one of them said. "He's up before four anyway."

"Who does the evening?" James asked.

They looked at each other. "I'll do it," said the youngest of the three, a man in his mid-thirties named Danny McClanahan who had the particular quality of someone who had been looking for a way to be useful since the first day and had not yet found the right one. "I know those roads better than anybody."

James believed him.

***

By the time the evening briefing ended he had the skeleton of something.

Not a plan exactly. Not yet. An architecture. The bones of a community response that could carry weight once the weight arrived. Eleven veterans committed to rotating watch positions. Two of Reeves's officers on the main road approach from the southeast. The McClanahan circuit running dawn and dusk. Roy Simmons's shortwave as a communication node. Tom Hargrove's managed inventory providing the community's most accurate picture of what it had and how long it would last.

He drove the perimeter himself after the briefing, the way he had been driving it every evening since Day 3. Not because he expected to find anything specific. Because driving it gave him the direct physical knowledge of the ground that no report or map could substitute for. He knew from experience that the difference between managing a situation from a desk and managing it from the actual terrain was the difference between understanding a problem and understanding how to solve it.

The farms in the dusk. The particular quality of the June evening light on the fields, long and golden and indifferent to everything human beings were doing in its presence. Cattle at the fence lines.

The Kowalski barn with its door properly latched. The Henderson property with a light in the kitchen window, a lantern or a candle, the warm specific glow of a house that was occupied and alert.

He was on his way back when he stopped.

He was passing the Miller farm on the eastern approach to Moores Hill. He had driven past it a dozen times in the past week and had noted it each time in the general inventory of the perimeter, a solid farm family, good land, situated far enough from the main road to be essentially invisible to anyone who did not already know it was there.

The farm lane leading back to the Miller property ran behind a long stand of mature trees. From the county road you could not see the house or the barn or the equipment. You could not see anything. If you did not already know the Miller farm was there, behind those trees at the end of that unmarked lane, you would drive past it without giving it a second thought.

James sat in his truck on the empty road with the engine running and looked at the unmarked lane and thought about the Henderson farm.

The Henderson farm was the Miller farm's nearest neighbor. The Henderson tools had gone missing on Day 5. Small tools. The kind of things you would take if you were making a preliminary assessment of an area, understanding what was available, before coming back for something more significant.

The Henderson farm was visible from the county road. The Miller farm was not.

James turned that over.

Someone had taken tools from the farm that was visible. They had also opened the barn door at the Kowalski place, which was visible from the road to the north. The Briggs truck had been taken from the property on the southeastern road, which was also visible.

Every targeted property had been visible from a county road.

Which meant the Miller farm, which was not visible from any county road, should not have been on anyone's list.

He sat with the engine idling and the last of the June light fading in the west and thought about the block party on Day 2. About the two men in Tom's hardware store on Day 1 with their eyes moving across the shelves. About the particular knowledge that a community watch position could acquire about the surrounding area simply by being present and observant over several days.

The Miller farm was not visible from the road.

But it was visible from the Henderson farm.

And anyone who had been on the Henderson property on Day 5, taking tools from an unlocked outbuilding, had been close enough to see the Miller barn through the tree line. Had been close enough to understand that there was something behind those trees that was not visible from the road. Had been close enough to make a note of it.

James looked at the unmarked lane for a long time.

Then he picked up the two-way radio Reeves had set him up with and called the Carnegie Hall basement.

"Reeves," he said.

"Here," Reeves said.

"Get Gary Whitfield," James said. "Tell him I need two people on the Miller farm lane tonight. Not visible from the road. Before full dark."

A pause. "You think tonight?"

"I think the Miller farm is on someone's list," James said. "And I think they know it's there."

He sat on the county road until he saw Gary Whitfield's truck turn off the main road toward the Miller farm. Watched it disappear down the lane behind the trees.

Then he turned around and drove back to Carnegie Hall.

There was more to do before he could sleep.

There was always more to do.

CHAPTER 5: THE ASHCRAFT CONVERSATION

The second week settled into Moores Hill the way serious things settle.

Not with drama. Not with a single moment that divided before from after. With the particular quiet weight of a situation that had stopped being temporary and had become, without anyone deciding it had, simply the way things were. People moved through their days with the adapted efficiency of those who had stopped waiting for the old normal to return and had started building a new one from what was available.

Carnegie Hall had become the community's center of gravity.

Not through any official designation. Through the same organic process that had filled it on the first day of the outage and had not stopped filling it since. People came for the morning briefings and stayed to talk. They came to use the tables by the windows where the light was good for the work that required light, letter writing and record keeping and the particular careful accounting of households that were managing finite resources with deliberate attention. They came because Margaret Hendricks was there with her camp stove coffee and her encyclopedic knowledge of Moores Hill and her quality of calm that seemed to function like a weather system, establishing the atmosphere of the room simply by being present in it.

Emma worked at her east window table every morning.

The custodian notebook had become the center of her investigative work in the same way Carnegie Hall had become the center of the community's life. Everything went into it. The estate records analysis. The Franklin Marsh thread. The observations she was building about the custodian network's silence and what the silence meant and what it required of her in the absence of the tools she had been using to build it. She wrote in the shorthand she had developed over three months of this work, a private notation system that was legible to her and to no one else, because a good investigator protected her working notes the same way she protected everything else of value.

Rufus slept under the table and occasionally rested his chin on her foot to confirm she was still there.

She had sent the two international letters ten days ago. She had sent the letter to Franklin Marsh eight days ago. She had no way of knowing whether any of them had arrived. She had no way of knowing whether the international mail was moving at all, or whether a letter sent from a small Indiana town during a regional grid failure had made it past the first distribution center. She had sent them into uncertainty and was managing the uncertainty the way she managed everything she could not control, by focusing on what she could.

What she could do was the physical records work.

She went to the historical society every afternoon. Dorothy Webb had established a routine around Emma's visits that involved having the relevant boxes pulled and ready when she arrived, which was an act of professional courtesy that Emma appreciated more than she said. The Caldwell estate files. The county property records from the relevant period. The Moores Hill College archives that touched on the Moore family history and the Carnegie Hall site. She worked through them with the focused patience of someone who understood that the answer was in the material and that the material would yield it if she looked carefully enough and for long enough.

She was two weeks into the patient work when Patricia Ashcraft walked into Carnegie Hall on a Wednesday morning and sat down across from her.

***

Emma had not seen her coming.

Not because she was not paying attention. Because Patricia Ashcraft had moved through the main hall of Carnegie Hall with the particular quality of someone who had made a decision and was carrying it toward its destination before she could reconsider it, walking with the direct purposefulness of a woman who had learned over decades of public life that hesitation in motion was its own kind of announcement.

She sat down across from Emma without preamble. Set her hands flat on the table. Looked at Emma with the expression of someone who has been rehearsing something and has decided, at the last moment, to abandon the rehearsed version and say the real thing instead.

"I need to tell you something," Patricia said. "I've been trying to figure out how to say it for months."

Emma set her pen down.

She had learned, in three months of investigative work and a lifetime of paying attention to people, that the correct response to this specific opening was silence. Not encouraging silence, not the murmured sounds that signaled keep going, just the plain absence of interruption that gave the other person the space to find their own way to what they needed to say. People who had been carrying something for months needed that space. They had already done the work of deciding to speak. What they needed now was room.

Patricia took a breath.

"My family has a box," she said. "We've had it for as long as anyone in the family can remember. Passed from parent to child, each generation, with instructions that were always the same. Don't open it. Keep it safe. When someone comes asking the right questions, you'll know."

She paused.

"My grandmother gave it to my mother the year before she died. My mother gave it to me when I turned forty. She said the same thing her mother had said to her. Don't open it. Keep it safe. You'll know when the time comes."

Emma looked at her steadily.

"I've had it in a closet in the mayoral residence for thirty years," Patricia said. "Thirty years. I've moved it three times. It has survived two floods and a burst pipe and a period when I genuinely considered throwing it away because I had decided the whole thing was family superstition dressed up as family tradition." She looked at her hands on the table. "I didn't throw it away."

"No," Emma said.

"No." Patricia looked up. "And then you came back to Moores Hill. And you started asking questions about Carnegie Hall and the history of the site and the Moore family and things that nobody had asked about in a very long time. And something happened that I did not expect."

Emma waited.

"I knew," Patricia said simply. "I didn't understand it. I still don't fully understand it. But I knew. The way my grandmother said I would know." She met Emma's eyes. "I think it's time to open the box."

***

Patricia brought it the following morning.

It was not what Emma had expected, though she had disciplined herself against expectation because expectation was the enemy of clear observation. She had thought, without fully forming the thought, of something ornate. Something that announced its significance through its appearance, carved or decorated or otherwise marked as a thing of importance.

The box was plain wood. Old wood, the grain darkened with age and handling, the surface worn smooth at the corners and edges where generations of hands had carried it. No markings on the outside. No lock. A simple fitted lid that had been made by someone who understood joinery well enough that it still seated perfectly despite however many years had passed since it was made.

Patricia set it on the table between them.

They both looked at it for a moment.

Then Patricia lifted the lid.

***

The smell reached Emma first. Something dry and mineral and very old, the smell of materials that had been enclosed for a long time in the particular suspended state that careful storage produced. Not decay. The opposite of decay. Preservation.

She looked at what was inside without touching anything.

Documents. Several of them, folded with care and stacked in a precise order that suggested someone had thought about the sequence in which they would be encountered. The paper was not modern paper. It had the texture and color of something made before paper became the standardized industrial product it was now, heavier and slightly irregular at the edges, the kind of paper that was made to last.

Beneath the documents, wrapped in a piece of cloth that had once been a color Emma could no longer identify with certainty, a set of small carved stone objects. She counted seven of them without lifting the cloth. Each one roughly the size of her palm. Each one carved with the same tool marks she had seen in the Carnegie Hall basement, on the ash circle markers that had been placed by hands that understood exactly what they were placing and why.

She recognized the work. She recognized it the way she had recognized the inscription in the Carnegie Hall basement the first time she saw it, with the particular quality of recognition that was not memory but something older than memory.

Beside the carved objects, a folded map.

She lifted it carefully by its edges and unfolded it on the table with the slow deliberateness of someone handling something that had survived a long time through careful handling and was not going to be the one to end that streak. The paper held. The folds opened along their original lines. She spread it flat and weighted the corners with her notebook and looked at what it showed.

Moores Hill. Or rather, the land that was now Moores Hill, rendered in a cartographic style that predated the town's founding by what she estimated, from the style and materials, was at least a century. Possibly more. The creek was there, running its actual course. The ridge lines. The particular topography of the land that the town had been built on and around.

And marked on it, in a notation system she did not immediately recognize but that she understood was a notation system, not decoration, a series of locations. Seven of them. Connected by lines that she had seen before, in a different form, in the Carnegie Hall basement. In Robert Moore's journal. In the architecture of the custodian network she had been building for three months.

She looked at the map for a long time without speaking.

Patricia sat across from her and waited with the patience of a woman who had been waiting thirty years and could wait a few minutes more.

"There's a letter," Emma said. She had seen it beneath the map, folded separately, the paper a slightly different weight and color from the documents.

"Yes," Patricia said.

Emma lifted it.

The outside was addressed in English, in handwriting that was precise and deliberate and belonged to someone who had taken the writing of this letter seriously. To whoever opens this box when the time comes. The date at the top of the letter was 1887.

She unfolded it and read.

***

The letter was three pages.

The handwriting was consistent throughout, the same careful precision from the first line to the last, no sign of the fatigue or haste that long handwritten documents usually accumulated. Whoever had written it had written it as a single sustained act of deliberate communication, something they had prepared for and taken seriously.

It began with the name.

Not Ashcraft. Ash-Craft. Hyphenated. With a brief explanation of the distinction that Emma read twice because the distinction mattered enormously.

The Ash-Craft families were the stonemason lineages of this region. Not stonemasons in the general sense of people who worked with stone. A specific tradition, a specific function, a specific knowledge that had been passed through the craft families of this area for generations that the letter writer estimated, cautiously, extended back further than written records could confirm. They were the people who had carved and placed and maintained the ash circle markers. The people who had kept the physical infrastructure of the Carnegie Hall site intact through the generations during which the ceremonial knowledge had been lost.

They had kept the name. They had not kept the mission. The letter writer was honest about this in a way that Emma found unexpectedly affecting. The knowledge of what the markers were and what they meant and what they were for had been broken. Colonization had broken it, the letter said, with the same plain factual tone it used for everything else, as if the magnitude of what was being described did not require embellishment. The transmission had been interrupted. The Ash-Craft families had continued maintaining the markers because maintaining the markers was what they did, because it was in the family practice, because no one had told them to stop, because stopping felt wrong even when no one alive could any longer explain why.

The letter writer had not recovered the full knowledge. They were honest about that too. What they had recovered, through a combination of the documents in the box and conversations with the last surviving person in their family who had carried fragments of the older understanding, was enough to know that the knowledge existed and that it would one day return to the site through a lineage that was not theirs.

The Moore lineage. Named in the letter with the specific recognition of someone who understood the custodian architecture well enough to know where the responsibility had gone when their own family's transmission failed.

The box, the letter explained, was to be kept until someone came asking the right questions. Not searching for it specifically. Asking the questions that only someone who had already found the knowledge would know to ask. At that point the Ash-Craft family's obligation was to open the box and to offer what it contained, because the knowledge it held belonged to the site and to the Moore lineage that served it, not to the family that had been keeping it.

The letter ended with a single sentence that Emma read three times.

We kept the markers. We could not keep the meaning. We trust that you will restore both.

***

Emma set the letter down on the table.

She was aware of Rufus under the table, his chin on her foot, the steady warm weight of him. She was aware of the sounds of Carnegie Hall going about its day around them, Margaret Hendricks's voice at the information table, the particular acoustic quality of the stone building absorbing and redistributing the sounds of the community inside it. She was aware of Patricia Ashcraft sitting across from her with an expression that had moved, over the course of the past hour, from the tense resolve of someone delivering something difficult to something quieter and harder to name.

"Patricia," Emma said.

"Yes."

"Do you know what's under this building?"

Patricia was quiet for a moment. Outside the east windows the morning light had moved, the direct angle of it shifting as the sun climbed, the quality of it changing from the sharp early light to the broader, warmer light of mid-morning.

"Not specifically," Patricia said. "I've known there was something. Since I was a child, actually, though I couldn't have told you what I knew or how I knew it. When the vote came up on the Carnegie Hall condemnation, the vote to demolish the building and sell the site for development, I sat in that meeting and listened to the arguments and they were reasonable arguments, practically speaking. The building needed significant restoration work. The site had commercial value. There were people in this community who needed what that commercial value could provide."

She paused.

"And I voted against it," she said. "I was the deciding vote. I voted against it and I could not tell you, if anyone had pressed me, exactly why. I had reasons. I gave the reasons. They were real reasons. But underneath them was something I couldn't put into words." She looked at the box. "Something in my blood remembered, I suppose. Even after all those generations of not knowing why."

Emma looked at her for a long moment.

Something in her blood remembered.

She thought about Linda, her mother, who had spent thirty five years protecting Carnegie Hall without knowing the full scope of what she was protecting, sustained by the same instinct that had sustained Patricia Ashcraft through a zoning vote that could have destroyed the site permanently. The instinct that outlasted the knowledge when the knowledge was broken. The inheritance that persisted in blood and bone and the particular felt sense of wrongness when the wrong thing was about to happen, even when the mind could no longer explain what made it wrong.

"The Ashcraft families," Emma said carefully. "The ones still in Moores Hill. Are there others?"

"Several," Patricia said. "Different branches. Most of them don't know each other particularly well. The name is the connection, and names don't explain themselves." She paused. "Why?"

Emma thought about the ash circle markers in the Carnegie Hall basement. About the inscription. About what it meant that the families who had placed and maintained those markers had never fully left the area, had been here all along, living in the town that had been built on and around the site they had been keeping without knowing they were keeping it.

"Because I think," Emma said slowly, "that the work of reconnecting this site to what it was is not something the Moore lineage does alone." She looked at the box. At the carved stone tools and the documents and the map and the letter that had been waiting in a closet for thirty years for exactly this conversation. "I think the Ash-Craft families were always supposed to be part of it. And I think finding out who they are and what they still carry, even without knowing they carry it, is something we need to do."

Patricia looked at her with the expression of someone receiving a thing they had been waiting for without knowing they were waiting for it.

"Tell me what you need," she said.

Outside Carnegie Hall the day went about its business. The community moved through its adapted routines. The summer heat pressed against the stone walls and the stone walls held it back. Rufus shifted under the table and resettled with a small sound of contentment.

Emma opened her custodian notebook to a fresh page and picked up her pen.

"Start at the beginning," she said. "Tell me everything you know about your family."

CHAPTER 6: THE PERIMETER HOLDS. BARELY.

The Miller farm incident happened on a Thursday night in the second week.

James had been expecting something. Not that specific farm on that specific night, but something, the escalation that the pattern had been pointing toward since the Henderson tools went missing on Day 5. He had positioned Gary Whitfield and two other veterans on rotating coverage of the Miller lane every night since he had sat on the county road and understood that someone knew the farm was there. Six nights of quiet. The circuit running at dawn and dusk without incident. The red and white cloth system working the way simple systems worked when they were designed correctly, which was without drama or failure.

On the seventh night the red cloth went up at the Miller fence post at two in the morning.

Danny McClanahan was doing the dusk-to-dawn circuit in his truck, the route he had been running every night since he volunteered for it at Sarah's diner, and he saw it in his headlights as he came around the bend on the county road. He did not stop. He kept moving at the same speed and called James on the two-way radio with the calm of someone who had been told exactly what to do in this situation and was doing it.

"Red cloth at Miller," Danny said.

"How long ago did you pass it on the dusk run?" James said.

"Seven hours," Danny said. "It was white at nine."

"Stay on the circuit," James said. "Don't come back to Miller."

He was already out of bed.

***

He called Gary Whitfield first. Gary was already awake. He had been awake since midnight with the particular alertness of someone whose instincts had been telling him something was wrong for two hours without being able to say what specifically was wrong.

"I've got two people on the lane," Gary said. "They haven't reported anything."

"They're not going in through the lane," James said. "Get to the eastern fence line. The creek drainage on the back of the property."

A pause. "You think they scouted it."

"I think they've been watching us watch the lane," James said. "Meet me at the Miller property line in fifteen minutes. Come in from the Henderson road, not the county road."

He called Reeves next. Two officers. Both of them. He told Reeves what he knew and what he suspected and what he needed and Reeves said ten minutes without asking questions that would have wasted time neither of them had.

He drove to the Miller farm in the dark with his lights off for the last half mile, navigating by the road's edge and the particular quality of the open sky above the fields that gave just enough ambient light to move by if you had been driving these roads long enough to know them in your body rather than just your eyes. He had been driving these roads for twelve years. He knew them.

He came in from the Henderson road the way he had told Gary to come in, the long way around that added eight minutes to the drive and kept him off the county road where anyone watching the Miller lane would have a sight line to approaching headlights.

***

There were eight of them.

James counted from the tree line at the eastern edge of the Miller property, lying flat on the ground with Gary beside him and Reeves's two officers positioned twenty meters to the south. Eight men moving across the back field in a spread formation that was not random. Someone had taught them this or they had learned it somewhere that taught people to move in fields at night without bunching up, without creating a single target, without losing sight of each other while maintaining enough separation to cover ground.

They were moving toward the equipment barn.

Not the house. Not the livestock. The equipment barn, which held the Miller family's generator and their fuel supply and the farm machinery that represented, in the current circumstances, the difference between a working farm and a property that could not sustain itself through the fall.

James watched them move and did his assessment.

Armed. He could see it in the way they carried themselves, the particular weight and posture of people who were moving with something on their hip or across their back that they were aware of. Not hunters, the equipment was wrong. People who had decided that the situation required being armed and had found the means to be armed and were now in a field in rural Indiana at two in the morning because someone had told them this farm had what they needed and had described the layout well enough for them to bypass the obvious entry point and come in through the creek drainage.

Someone had described the layout.

James filed that and stayed still.

He waited until they were thirty meters from the equipment barn, committed enough to their approach that turning back required a decision rather than simply a change of direction, and then he stood up and turned on the flashlight he had brought for exactly this moment, the large one with the beam that carried, and Gary stood up beside him and the two officers stood up to the south.

"Dearborn County Sheriff," James said. His voice carried across the field the way voices carried across open ground at night, clearly and without effort. "Stop where you are."

They stopped.

The moment that followed had a quality James recognized from experience. The specific held breath of a situation that had not yet decided what it was going to be, that was balanced between the several things it could become, and that would tip one way or another based on what happened in the next ten seconds.

He kept the flashlight on them and did not move.

Eight men standing in a field at two in the morning, thirty meters from what they had come to take, looking at four people with lights and the particular posture of people who were not going to move.

The decision traveled through them visibly. James watched it happen the way he had watched decisions travel through groups before. Not a conversation. Something faster than conversation, a collective assessment conducted in the space of a few seconds through the particular communication of people who are in a situation together and understand simultaneously what the situation is.

Six of them put their hands up.

Two of them ran.

James let them run. He had Reeves's officers and he had Gary and he had the two veterans who had been on the lane and who had moved to the southern fence line when they got his call, and he had six people standing in a field with their hands in the air, and running after two people in the dark across ground he did not know as well as they apparently did was not a calculation that made sense.

"On the ground," James said to the six. "Hands where I can see them."

They went to the ground.

***

It took two hours to sort out.

Reeves arrived twenty minutes after the initial confrontation with his remaining officer and a set of zip ties that he had been carrying in his vehicle since Day 3 for reasons he had not explained to anyone and that James appreciated without asking about. The six men were secured and moved to the Carnegie Hall basement, which had become, by the practical necessity of the situation, the closest thing Moores Hill had to a holding facility.

James sat with them one at a time.

What he learned over those two hours he sorted carefully. In his experience, people in difficult circumstances said three kinds of things: what was true, what they thought you wanted to hear, and what they hoped might help their situation. The trick was knowing which was which. He had been doing it long enough to know.

They were from Cincinnati. A neighborhood on the western edge of the city that James knew from his law enforcement contacts as an area that had been struggling before the outage and was now, by the accounts he was hearing, operating in a state of significant organized desperation. They had not come on their own initiative. Someone had organized this. Someone had identified Moores Hill as a target, had gathered information about the community's resources and layout, and had sent these eight men out with enough information to get to the Miller farm's back fence line.

That information had not come from observation alone.

James knew this the way he knew the things his experience had made available to him, with a certainty that preceded the specific evidence and that he understood was not yet evidence itself. The Henderson tools missing on Day 5. The Kowalski barn door on Day 6. Six days of watching the community's perimeter and the community's routines and the community's patterns before the Miller farm attempt. That was a reconnaissance operation, conducted methodically over nearly two weeks, by people who understood what reconnaissance was for.

But reconnaissance from the outside had limits. You could learn what was visible. You could learn patterns if you watched long enough. What you could not learn, from the outside, was the specific internal geography of a farm that was not visible from any road.

Someone had told them about the creek drainage.

James thanked the six men for their cooperation and left them in the Carnegie Hall basement with Reeves and went upstairs to find a corner where he could sit alone for a few minutes and think about who in Moores Hill had known about the Miller farm's creek drainage and who that person might have told.

***

The community vote on the formal perimeter closure happened three days later.

James had been working toward it since the Miller farm incident, not because he had decided it was the right answer before the community had a chance to decide, but because the Miller farm incident had changed the information the community was working with and a community that was working with new information deserved the opportunity to make a new decision.

He presented it at the evening briefing without editorializing. What had happened at the Miller farm. What it indicated about the level of organization developing outside the community. What a formal perimeter closure would mean in practical terms. What it would require from the people who had been staffing the watch positions. What it would mean for anyone who wanted to enter or leave Moores Hill for any reason.

He also presented the argument against it, because he was not interested in running a meeting that arrived at a predetermined conclusion. There were people in Moores Hill who believed, and believed sincerely, that a community with food had a moral obligation to share it with people who did not. That closing the perimeter was a decision to prioritize the survival of this specific community over the survival of people who had the misfortune of not living in it. That the arithmetic of what Moores Hill had and how long it would last was not the only arithmetic that mattered.

James thought that argument deserved to be heard in full before the vote, because the people making it were not wrong that it was an argument worth making. They were reaching a different conclusion than he was reaching from the same facts, and the difference was not stupidity or selfishness on either side. It was a genuine disagreement about what a community owed the people outside it when resources were finite and the outside was pressing in.

The vote passed. Not unanimously.

Seven people voted against the closure. James noted who they were, not with suspicion, but because in a community managing a crisis, understanding where the disagreements were was as important as understanding where the agreements were. The seven people who voted against the closure were not a problem. They were members of the community who had expressed a sincere position through the available process and had been outvoted and had sat down and accepted it.

He respected that. He also watched, carefully and without broadcasting that he was watching, to make sure that the position remained expressed through words and votes and not through other means.

***

He took the overnight shift at the main entrance himself three nights a week.

He had told the community he was doing this and he had been honest about why. He had asked people to staff positions that were uncomfortable and tiring and that required them to be present and alert during the hours when alertness was hardest to maintain. He was not going to ask that of his people without doing it himself. That was the kind of thing that was not negotiable for James McClanahan, the same way certain other things were not negotiable, and the community understood it about him well enough that no one had commented on it.

The main entrance overnight was quiet most nights.

Not empty. There was traffic on the county road at hours that surprised him. People moving in the dark, alone or in small groups, on foot or on bicycle, with the particular directed energy of people who had somewhere to be and had decided that darkness was a reasonable time to be getting there. He stopped most of them. Talked to them. Assessed each situation on its own terms and made individual decisions rather than applying a rule uniformly, because uniform rules were appropriate for normal circumstances and these were not normal circumstances and the person in front of him on any given night was a specific person in a specific situation that deserved a specific response.

Most of them he turned back. Some of them he let through. One family, a mother and two children who had walked from a neighborhood east of Cincinnati and who were trying to reach a grandmother in Aurora, he drove to Aurora himself at four in the morning because the grandmother's address was eight miles in the wrong direction for walking and the children were eight and eleven years old and it was the right thing to do.

He was back at the entrance by six.

On the third overnight shift, in the small hours of a Thursday morning, a vehicle appeared on the county road with its lights off.

James saw it before his watch partner did, the dark shape of it moving on the road without the headlights that a vehicle moving on a county road at three in the morning should have had, and he felt something shift in his assessment of the situation in the way that things shifted when experience was reading something before the conscious mind had caught up with what it was reading.

"Vehicle," he said quietly. "Lights off. Coming slow."

His watch partner, Gary Whitfield, was already tracking it.

They stepped into the road. Gary had the large flashlight. James had his hand on the radio. They flagged the vehicle down with the standard signals they had established for exactly this situation and the vehicle stopped twenty meters from the checkpoint.

James approached from the side with the flashlight covering the driver's window.

There was no driver.

The vehicle was a late model pickup truck, engine running, in gear, moving on the county road at three in the morning with no one behind the wheel. He processed that for one second, the specific second in which his experience told him what it meant before his mind had finished forming the question, and then he was already turning and already reaching for the radio.

"All positions," he said into the radio. "This is a distraction. Report in. Report in now."

The positions reported in, one by one, the watch voices coming through with the quick professional brevity of people who had been trained to communicate under pressure.

Henderson road, clear.

Kowalski approach, clear.

Southern entrance, clear.

Then: "Miller farm. Miller farm, we've got a problem. Generator's gone."

James stood on the county road with the empty truck still idling twenty meters away and felt the cold specific clarity of someone who has just understood that they have been outmaneuvered.

Not beaten. Not broken. Outmaneuvered. By people who were learning from the previous attempt the way his people were learning from it, who had understood that the lane and the fence line were watched now and had found a different approach, who had understood that the main entrance checkpoint was the community's most visible security position and had used that visibility against it.

He thought about the creek drainage. About the internal knowledge that had gotten eight men to the back of the Miller property two weeks ago. About the specific person or persons who had provided that knowledge and who were apparently still providing it.

The game had changed.

He called Gary over and told him to stay with the truck. Documented vehicle. No one touches it until Reeves gets here.

Then he drove to the Miller farm.

The generator was gone. Not damaged. Not disabled. Removed, with the efficiency of people who had come prepared to remove it, who had the equipment and the knowledge of what they were taking and had done it in the window of time that the distraction on the county road had purchased them.

Twelve minutes. The entire operation had taken twelve minutes.

James stood in the Miller equipment barn in the pre-dawn dark and looked at the empty space where the generator had been and thought about the twelve minutes and what twelve minutes of organized, coordinated action required in terms of planning and preparation and inside knowledge.

He drove back to Carnegie Hall.

Reeves was already there, having come from the county road where the truck had been secured. He looked at James when James came through the door with the particular expression of someone who understood that the conversation they were about to have was going to be a difficult one.

"Someone told them," Reeves said.

"Yes," James said.

"One of ours."

"Yes," James said.

He sat down at the basement desk and looked at the map on the wall and thought about the seven people who had voted against the perimeter closure and the people who had staffed the watch positions and the people who knew the farm circuit schedule and the people who had been in the room when the Miller farm was discussed and the specific overlapping set of all of those categories.

He thought about who was in that overlap.

He began, in the careful methodical way he began everything that required methodical care, to make a list.

He did not write it down.

He kept it in his head, the way he kept things that were not ready to be committed to paper, and he went over it and refined it and added to it and reduced it until what remained was a direction.

Not a name yet.

A direction.

He would follow it.

CHAPTER 7: THE PAPER TRAIL

The letter came back on a Tuesday.

Emma found it in Gerald Sims's incoming stack when she stopped at the post office on her way to the historical society, her name on the front in her own handwriting, the envelope slightly battered from whatever journey it had made before turning around and coming home. Gerald handed it to her with the expression of a man delivering bad news that was not his fault and that he had been unable to prevent.

"Cincinnati return," he said. "Came back on yesterday's run from Lawrenceburg. The postal service there says delivery in the city is operating sporadically. Some addresses are getting mail. Some aren't."

Emma looked at the envelope. The Franklin Marsh address on Montgomery Road had been one of the ones that wasn't.

"Thank you Gerald," she said.

She put the letter in her bag and walked to Carnegie Hall and found James in the basement.

"I need to go to Cincinnati," she said.

James looked up from the perimeter map, which had acquired new notations since the Miller farm incident and the generator theft. He looked at her with the assessing quality he brought to requests that had implications beyond the request itself.

"How long?" he said.

"Half a day. There and back. I need to find someone in person."

"The father thread," James said. It was not a question.

"Yes."

He was quiet for a moment. "The city is different from what it was. People coming out of Cincinnati at the checkpoint describe something that's gotten harder in the past week. It's not chaos. It's the thing that comes after the initial chaos settles into structure."

"I understand," Emma said.

"Take Rufus," James said. "Be back before dark." He looked at her for a moment. "Find what you're looking for."

***

The drive to Cincinnati took an hour and ten minutes instead of forty because of what James had described as structure. Not chaos. Caravans. Small groups moving together on the county roads with a purposefulness that was different from the individual and desperate movement of the early days. People who had figured out that moving alone was dangerous and had found others to move with. She let most of them pass or moved around them carefully. An etiquette had developed on those roads, the particular social negotiation of people sharing a resource that required cooperation to use safely.

Rufus sat in the passenger seat and watched the caravans with professional interest.

The suburban ring announced itself first, the infrastructure of American consumer life all of it dark and closed. Parking lots empty. Drive-throughs blocked with hand-lettered signs. A gas station with a line of vehicles extending down the block and around the corner, people waiting for something that was not yet available but that someone had apparently suggested might become available.

Then the city proper.

The streets were not empty. That was the first thing that surprised her. People moving on foot and bicycle and the occasional vehicle in patterns that were purposeful rather than casual, the movement of people going somewhere specific for a reason rather than the ambient movement of a functioning city going about its ordinary business. Generators hummed from hospital windows. A police cruiser parked at an intersection, two officers inside doing the visible work of being present.

The grocery stores were what stopped her breath.

She passed two of them on the route to Montgomery Road. Both locked. Both with the particular emptied quality visible through the windows at a distance, shelves that had been full three weeks ago now showing the pale institutional color of empty shelving units all the way to the back wall. Not primarily looted. Simply bought. The supply chain that restocked those shelves every forty-eight hours had stopped and the shelves showed it.

She found Montgomery Road and found the building.

***

Franklin Marsh's office occupied the ground floor of a narrow three-story building on a block that had been commercial on the ground level and residential above it. The office windows were dark. A hand-lettered sign on the door said CLOSED UNTIL FURTHER NOTICE.

Emma knocked anyway.

Nothing.

She looked at the building. A curtain moved on the second floor, the specific small movement of someone checking who was at the door without committing to answering it. She stepped back so she was visible from the second-floor window and held up the letter she had written, her name on the return address visible, and waited.

Sixty seconds. Then footsteps on interior stairs. Then the door opened.

Franklin Marsh was in his mid-seventies, shorter than she had imagined from his name, with the physical quality of a man who had been vigorous into his later years and was now operating on the momentum of that earlier vigor rather than its current presence. He looked at her with the careful assessment of someone who had been managing his own threshold for three weeks.

He looked at Rufus.

"The dog stays outside," he said.

"He goes where I go," Emma said.

Marsh looked at Rufus, who was sitting with the composed patience he brought to all situations that required waiting and who was looking back at Marsh with no particular expression.

"Fine," Marsh said. "Come in."

***

The office had the smell of a space that had been lived in unexpectedly. A cot visible through a half-open interior door. A camp stove on the credenza. The accumulated evidence of someone who had been sleeping and eating in a professional space because the professional space was where they happened to be when everything changed.

Marsh sat behind his desk. Emma sat across from it. Rufus settled between them with his chin on his paws.

"You mentioned the Caldwell estate at the door," Marsh said. "That's not a name I hear often." He looked at her with the careful assessment of a man who had spent forty years reading people across a desk. "Who are you and what's your interest in it?"

"My name is Emma Caldwell," she said. "I'm a researcher with an interest in the family's connections to Moores Hill's early history. Robert Caldwell had ties to the town that I've been trying to document."

Marsh was quiet, sitting with that the way lawyers sat with things.

"Researchers usually come with institutional affiliations," he said. "Universities. Law firms. Historical societies." He looked at her. "You didn't mention one."

"I'm an independent researcher," Emma said.

"I remember the Caldwell estate," he said finally. "I would have remembered it regardless, because most estates blur together in the way that routine work blurs. The Caldwell estate did not blur."

"Why not?" Emma said. Though she already knew part of the answer.

Marsh leaned back in his chair. "In my experience, the administration of an estate begins when the attorney is engaged. There is a period of gathering documentation. Death certificate. Will, if one exists. Property records. Financial account information. The various pieces of a life that have to be assembled before the legal process of distributing that life's assets can begin."

He paused.

"When I was engaged to handle the Caldwell estate, the documentation was already assembled. Complete. Organized in a manner that suggested significant preparation. Not the preparation of a man who had made careful arrangements for his own eventual death. The preparation of someone who had assembled these documents recently, deliberately, in anticipation of a specific event."

Emma kept her face still. "What kind of event?"

"The death," Marsh said simply. He looked at her with the direct clarity of a man who had been sitting with this observation for twenty-three years and had decided, in the strange freedom of a world that had lost its normal rules for a while, to say it plainly. "The documentation was prepared before the death occurred. The paper had the wrong relationship with the timeline."

Outside the office window Cincinnati went about its adapted day. Quieter than it should have been, the ambient noise of urban life reduced to something that revealed the sounds underneath it. Birds. A creek running through the neighborhood, audible in a way it was not audible normally.

Emma thought about Moores Hill and the creek behind Oak Street.

"Did you raise concerns at the time?" she said.

"I mentioned it to a colleague," Marsh said. "Informally. He suggested I was reading significance into coincidence." He looked at his hands on the desk. "I filed it. I completed the estate administration, which was straightforward because everything was already in order, and I collected my fee and moved on to the next matter."

"But you didn't forget it," Emma said.

"No," Marsh said. "I didn't forget it." He looked at her. "You're not a historian."

"No," Emma said.

"You're connected to the family."

It was not a question. Emma met his eyes.

"Robert Caldwell was my father," she said. "He was reported dead when I was eight years old. I have reason to believe the report was false."

The room was quiet.

Marsh looked at her for a long moment with the expression of a man receiving confirmation of something he had suspected for twenty-three years and finding that confirmation was both more and less satisfying than he had imagined it would be.

"There's something else," Marsh said.

Emma waited.

"I don't often think about that estate anymore. But you're sitting across from me asking about it and something is telling me I should show you this." He pushed back from the desk and went to the filing cabinet against the wall. He opened the bottom drawer and searched through it with the unhurried patience of a man who kept his records in a system only he fully understood. After a minute he found what he was looking for and brought it back to the desk.

A folder, old and slightly yellowed at the edges. He placed it between them.

"The original Caldwell estate file," he said. "I kept a copy. Longer than I'm required to, because I have always believed that the value of a record is not always apparent at the time it is made."

Emma looked at the folder.

"There are three things absent from this file that should be present in any estate of this complexity," Marsh said. "I noticed them at the time." He told her what they were.

Each one was exactly what Emma had identified in the county records. The same three absences. Arrived at independently, twenty-three years apart, by two people looking at the same estate documentation from different directions.

"Someone with significant legal authority shaped this estate," Emma said.

"Yes," Marsh said. "Someone who knew exactly what they were doing and exactly what they needed the record to show and not show." He paused. "I never identified who. I suspected it was someone with access to the filing infrastructure at the county level, but I had no way to confirm it and no standing to investigate."

Emma thought about the name she had written in her custodian notebook.

"One more question," she said.

"Yes," Marsh said.

"In your professional opinion, as someone who has administered estates for forty years, is what you've described consistent with a man faking his own death?"

Marsh was quiet for a long moment.

"In my professional opinion," he said carefully, "it is not inconsistent with it."

***

She drove back to Moores Hill in the late afternoon with the folder on the passenger seat beside Rufus.

The road home was quieter than the road in. She passed the suburban ring and the county roads and the farms and drove through the June evening light that made the Indiana landscape look the way it always looked at this hour, timeless and unhurried.

She thought about a man who had assembled a folder of documents before his own death and handed it to a Cincinnati lawyer and had walked away from his family and had been walking away ever since. She thought about what that cost. She thought about what it said about what he believed he was protecting them from that the cost had seemed worth it.

She pulled into Moores Hill as the light was going gold and parked in front of her house and sat in the truck for a moment.

Then she went inside and opened her custodian notebook to the page where she had written Find Franklin Marsh

She drew a single line through it.

Below it she wrote three new words.

Her father was alive.

She looked at the words for a long moment. Then she turned the page and started writing everything she knew, from the beginning, in the careful complete way she wrote things that needed to be preserved exactly as they were before the next step changed them.

The investigation had arrived somewhere new.

So had she.

CHAPTER 8: THE COLLABORATOR

James had been keeping a list for three weeks.

Not on paper. In his head, in the particular mental space he reserved for things that were not ready to be written down, things still being assembled, still being tested against the available evidence, still carrying enough uncertainty that committing them to paper felt like a conclusion he had not yet earned the right to reach.

He had started it the morning after the Miller farm generator theft. After he had stood in the equipment barn in the pre-dawn dark and understood that twelve minutes of coordinated action required planning and preparation and inside knowledge, and had driven back to Carnegie Hall and begun to think about who.

Not who specifically. Who in what category. Who had access to what information and when. Who had been in the room during which conversations. Who had known about the farm circuit schedule and the watch rotation and the specific internal geography of properties not visible from any public road.

The farm circuit schedule. Twelve people had been in the room when Danny McClanahan described the route at Sarah's diner on Day 7. The watch rotation. Sixteen people had direct knowledge of which positions were staffed at which hours. The internal geography of the Miller farm, specifically the creek drainage on the eastern boundary that the first group of eight had used as their approach. This was the constraint that mattered most. You could not see the creek drainage from any road. You had to have been on the property or been told by someone who had.

James knew every person who had been on the Miller farm in the past month. He had asked Bill Miller directly, framed as routine community resource assessment, and Bill had given him seven names without hesitation.

Seven names. Against both other lists. The overlap was three people.

James was one of them.

He looked at the other two.

***

He watched them for ten days.

Not obtrusively. He simply added them to the things he paid attention to during his normal movement through Moores Hill, which was extensive enough that paying attention to two additional people required no special adjustment.

He was looking for pattern disruption. The specific behavioral changes that occurred when a person was managing something in addition to what everyone else was managing, the particular quality of someone carrying an additional weight the people around them could not see.

The first person gave him nothing. Present at briefings, engaged in conversations, pulling their weight on the watch rotation without complaint. The normal variations of someone going through a difficult period, nothing that distinguished them from any of the other people in Moores Hill carrying the same weight. He crossed them off the list at the end of the first week.

The second person was different.

Not dramatically. That was the thing about it that stayed with James and that he turned over repeatedly in the evenings. The difference was not dramatic. It was the kind of difference that you could dismiss individually and that accumulated over ten days into something that could no longer be dismissed.

The way they listened in rooms had changed. Not their level of engagement. The quality of it. There was a difference, subtle but present, between the listening of someone interested in a conversation and the listening of someone who needed to know what was being said. The first kind had a relaxed receptiveness. The second kind had a focus that was slightly too consistent, tracking specific information rather than the natural flow of exchange.

James had seen that kind of listening before in contexts where it had mattered.

He watched it show up in the morning briefings. In the farm resource meetings. In the casual conversations at Margaret Hendricks's information table that were not official briefings but that contained exactly the kind of operational detail that someone feeding information outward would want to capture.

He watched them leave the evening briefing on Day 16 and take a route home that went three blocks out of their way for no reason James could identify.

He said nothing to anyone.

He needed one more piece before he moved.

***

The Kowalski farm was hit on a Wednesday morning.

Not the barn this time. The smokehouse, which Steve Kowalski had been using to preserve the pork from two hogs he had processed the previous week. Weeks of protein for a farm family managing a long outage. The smokehouse was behind the main barn, not visible from the county road, not visible from the farm lane, visible only from the back of the property or from the adjacent Henderson field.

James had told three people about the Kowalski smokehouse.

He had mentioned it in the context of the community food resource inventory, as an example of preservation capability the community should factor into its planning. He had mentioned it in a conversation conducted deliberately, with deliberate specificity, with the three people on his overlap list, at three separate times, in three separate conversations, so that he would know, if the smokehouse was targeted, which conversation had mattered.

He had been telling himself he was wrong for ten days. He had constructed the test because he needed the result to be definitive before he could act on it, and part of him had been hoping, in the honest place underneath the investigation, that the test would come back negative.

The smokehouse was hit.

James sat in the Carnegie Hall basement with that result and let himself feel the full weight of it for exactly as long as it deserved. Then he stood up and went to make an arrangement.

***

He found them at home.

Mid-afternoon. He knocked on the door.

They answered it with the expression of someone who had been expecting, without admitting to themselves they were expecting it, exactly this visit. Not surprise. The specific emotional state of someone for whom a dreaded thing has finally arrived and who is experiencing, alongside the dread, the particular exhausted relief of a burden that has been carried alone for a long time and is about to be set down.

"Can I come in?" James said.

They stepped back from the door.

***

He sat across from them at their kitchen table and did not say anything for a moment. The kitchen had the particular adapted quality of all Moores Hill kitchens in the third week of the outage, camp stove on the counter, candles staged for the evening, the domestic reorganization of a household managing finite resources with deliberate attention. A child's drawing on the refrigerator, held by a magnet from a vacation that felt like it belonged to a different era.

James looked at the drawing and then at the person across from him.

"Tell me," he said. That was all.

What came out was not what he had expected.

He had expected denial first. He had prepared for denial and had prepared what came after denial.

There was no denial.

They broke in the particular way of someone who has been holding something alone for too long and has finally been given permission to put it down. Not gradually. All at once, the way things broke when the structure holding them had been under maximum load for an extended period.

The contact had come in the second week. A man at the checkpoint on the county road, not one of the eight from the Miller farm incident, someone different, someone who had presented himself as a community liaison from a neighborhood organization in Cincinnati trying to establish resource-sharing agreements with rural communities. The language had been reasonable. The framing had been cooperative. James noted that detail and filed it. Whoever was organizing this was sophisticated enough to lead with language that sounded like negotiation rather than threat.

The refusal had been immediate and genuine.

And then their daughter had not come home from a supply run to Lawrenceburg.

James was quiet when that part of the story arrived. He let it settle completely before he said anything.

Three weeks ago. A note slipped under the back door in the night. Handwritten. One page. The terms laid out without ambiguity and the consequences of non-compliance described with the same plain clarity.

A dead drop. Behind the grain elevator on the eastern county road. Information left there by the collaborator. Proof of life left in return. Every four days, without fail, in both directions.

Three weeks of it. Three weeks of walking to that grain elevator in the dark and leaving what had been asked for and finding in its place a photograph. Always a photograph. Their daughter holding a handwritten date to prove it was current. Frightened but unharmed.

The next exchange was in two days.

James sat at the kitchen table and felt the full complicated weight of the situation settle into its actual shape, which was not the shape he had been carrying in his mental list for three weeks. The shape in his mental list had been simpler. Betrayal was simpler. What was sitting across from him was a parent who had been told their child would die and had made the only calculation available to them.

He did not say anything for a long time after they finished.

The child's drawing on the refrigerator. A house with a sun above it and two figures in front of it, the particular style of children who drew people as circles on sticks, full of confidence in the representation regardless of its relationship to literal accuracy. He looked at it and thought about three weeks of walking to that grain elevator in the dark. The specific texture of it. The way each exchange would have been the only thing that mattered in the four days leading up to it and the only thing that mattered in the four days after.

He thought about what a person would do to keep those photographs coming.

"You're going to keep cooperating," he said finally. "Exactly as you have been. And you're going to tell me everything they've asked for and everything you've told them." He paused. "And in two days when that exchange happens, I'm going to be there."

They looked at him with the expression of someone who has been carrying something alone for three weeks in the dark and has just been told they no longer have to carry it alone, and the relief of that was complicated by everything else the moment contained.

"Can you get her back?" they said.

James looked at them steadily.

"I'm going to try," he said.

It was the most honest answer he had. It was also, he understood from the way they received it, exactly the right answer. Not a promise. Not a reassurance. The plain truth of what he was committing to, offered without decoration, from someone who did not make commitments lightly and who they could see, sitting across the kitchen table from them in the afternoon light, understood the full weight of the one he had just made.

"Tell me everything," James said. "From the beginning. Leave nothing out."

They told him.

He listened with the complete attention he brought to everything that mattered, and he did not interrupt, and he did not reach for his notebook because this was not the moment for a notebook, and when they finished he sat quietly for a moment and then began, in the careful methodical way he began everything, to think about what came next.

Outside the kitchen window Moores Hill went about its afternoon. A daughter still out there.

James thought about that.

Then he stood up, thanked them for telling him, and went back to Carnegie Hall to find Reeves.

There was work to do.

***

She had stopped counting the hours somewhere in the second day.

Not because she had given up on tracking time. Because the grain facility had no windows in the section where they kept her and the difference between day and night was only the quality of the sounds from outside, birds in the morning that she could identify by type if she concentrated, and the particular silence of deep night that was different from the silence of midday in a way she could not have explained but that she felt in her body with the specific accuracy of someone who had been paying very close attention to the only information available to her.

She had decided on the first night that paying attention was the job.

Not panicking. Not crying more than she could help. Not doing anything that used energy she did not know how to replace. Paying attention. Cataloguing. Counting what she knew and what she did not know and what she could control and what she could not.

What she knew: there were two of them and they did not speak to each other in front of her and they brought food twice a day and the food was not generous but it was consistent and consistent meant they needed her to stay functional which meant they were not going to let her die.

What she did not know: why. She did not know why and she had stopped trying to figure out why because figuring out why required information she did not have and the attempt to figure it out without the information only produced fear and fear used energy she needed for something else.

What she could control: almost nothing. She had found the edges of the space they had given her on the first night by moving slowly in the dark with her hands out until she had mapped it completely. Twelve feet by fourteen feet approximately. A concrete floor. A metal wall on two sides and a wooden partition on the other two. A bucket. A sleeping pad that smelled of grain and age. A blanket that was not warm enough.

She pulled the blanket around her shoulders and listened to the silence of midday in the grain facility and thought about her parents.

She did not let herself think about them for long.

That was the other thing she had decided. Thinking about her parents used the kind of energy that did not come back. She allowed herself thirty seconds of it in the morning and thirty seconds at night and then she put it away and went back to paying attention.

Thirty seconds was enough to remember why she was doing this.

She folded the blanket more tightly and sat with her back against the metal wall and waited for the afternoon feeding and listened to the facility around her and paid attention.

CHAPTER 9: THE LETTER ARRIVES

The mail run to Lawrenceburg happened every Tuesday and Friday.

Danny McClanahan drove it, the same Danny who ran the farm circuit at dusk, because Danny had turned out to be the kind of person who filled available roles without being asked twice and who treated every task he took on with the same focused reliability regardless of whether the task was glamorous. The mail run was not glamorous. Forty minutes each direction on county roads that were quieter than they used to be but not without their own complications, coordination with Gerald Sims on both ends, results that were unpredictable in the specific way that all mail was unpredictable during a period when the system holding it together was operating on improvisation and goodwill.

Emma checked the incoming stack every Tuesday and Friday without fail. She arrived at Gerald's counter within an hour of Danny's return, looked through the incoming for anything addressed to her Carnegie Hall address, and found most weeks nothing. The ordinary correspondence of investigative work moving at the pace that investigative work moved when its infrastructure had been reduced to paper and human drivers.

She was not impatient. But she was aware, in the careful part of her mind that tracked the status of every open thread, that six weeks had passed since she sent two letters to addresses on other continents.

On a Tuesday morning in the seventh week she arrived at Gerald's counter and Gerald handed her an envelope without being asked.

"This one's yours," he said. "Came in on this morning's run."

The envelope was not standard American postal stock. Slightly larger and slightly heavier, the paper with a different texture, the kind of envelope that was ordinary in some parts of the world and slightly unusual in others. Her Carnegie Hall address written in handwriting that was careful and deliberate, the letters formed with the particular precision of someone writing in a language that was not their first but that they had learned thoroughly. A European postmark. A post office box return address with no city name, no country, no identifying information beyond the number itself.

She thanked Gerald and put the envelope in her bag and walked to Carnegie Hall without opening it.

***

She sat at her east window table.

Rufus settled under the table with the immediacy of a dog who understood that his person had received something significant and that the appropriate response was to be present and still.

She opened the envelope carefully. Not from anxiety. From the recognition that this was something that deserved to be opened with attention rather than haste.

The letter was four pages. Handwritten on both sides of two sheets of the same paper as the envelope, in the same careful deliberate script. She looked at the signature at the end of the fourth page before she read the letter itself, the way she looked at the source of any document before reading its contents.

The signature was a family name she recognized from Robert Moore's journals. A name she had been hoping to see and had not been certain she would.

She turned back to the beginning and read.

***

The letter opened with an acknowledgment that her letter had arrived, and with an apology for the delay in responding that attributed the delay to the difficulty of knowing what to say rather than the difficulty of the postal situation, though both had played a role. The family had received her letter and had read it several times and had discussed it at length before deciding how to respond, and the response had been rewritten twice before this version had been committed to the envelope.

She understood that. She had rewritten her own letter several times.

The first substantial section addressed the Montana sealing.

They had felt it. That was the word they used, felt, without apology or qualification, in the plain matter-of-fact way that people described experiences that were real to them regardless of whether the language available to describe them was adequate. They had been aware of something changing in the network at the moment of the sealing in a way that had been unmistakable to them. They had understood it as a significant event. They had not known its source until her letter arrived.

She read that section twice.

Then she read the section about Carnegie Hall.

What the letter contained about the Carnegie Hall site went beyond what Robert Moore's journals had documented. Not contradicting the journals. Supplementing them, filling in aspects of the site's history and significance that the journals had not addressed, in ways that suggested the family's documentation of the network came from sources that predated Moore's own research and had been maintained independently across a different part of the world for a very long time.

Specific details. The orientation of the ceremonial space relative to the seven sites. A description of the inscription in the basement that matched, word for word, what Emma had found there, written in a document that had been in this family's possession for generations before Moore's College was built above it. The particular quality of the Carnegie Hall site's relationship to the Montana site, which the letter described as complementary rather than parallel, two nodes in the network designed to function in relationship to each other in ways that neither could achieve independently.

Emma's hands were not entirely steady by the time she finished that section.

She set the letter down for a moment and looked out the east window at Main Street going about its morning and felt the particular quality of receiving confirmation that something you believed was true had been true all along, which was not simple relief but something more complicated that included the weight of what the confirmation meant and included the specific loneliness of understanding something that most of the people around you would not understand and were not equipped to understand.

Rufus put his chin on her foot.

She picked the letter up and continued.

The third section addressed her specifically, her work, what the letter characterized as the restoration effort, the reconnection of the network that had been broken by colonization and that was, in the family's assessment, further along than anything they had seen in their own lifetime of maintaining their part of it. They wrote about this with something closer to relief than praise. The specific relief of people who had been maintaining something alone for a very long time and had just learned that someone else was doing the same work from a different direction.

She understood that quality. She had been feeling a version of it herself since the moment she found her mother's journal in the attic.

Then the final paragraph.

The paragraph discussed the broader landscape of the work. The family's understanding of who was involved in maintaining the network beyond the custodian lineages themselves. There were others, the letter said. People who had come to the sites through different paths and had dedicated significant portions of their lives to the work without carrying the bloodline that made the custodian role specific. Some of these people were known to the family. Some were not known to them but were known to exist through the traces they left in the network's history.

And then the sentence.

We are not alone in our work. There are others who have dedicated their lives to the sites outside the custodian lineages. Some of them you will come to know. Some of them you may already know without realizing it.

Emma set the letter down on the table.

She thought about the ghost pattern in the missing persons databases. Twenty years of searches keyed to the same coordinates she had been searching, conducted by someone who had built a sophisticated monitoring infrastructure around the seven sites and had been running it with the patient consistency of someone who understood what they were watching and why it mattered.

She thought about the three absences in the Caldwell estate record. About Franklin Marsh saying the documentation was prepared before the death occurred. About Gerald Forsythe's financial accounts and the name that was not Robert Caldwell registered under a structure built with the deliberate patience of someone who intended it to last.

She thought about her father.

The sentence did not say what she was reading into it. She was aware of that. She was reading a specific meaning into language general enough to carry several meanings, and the investigation she had been conducting for seven weeks had primed her to read it that way, and she needed to be honest with herself about that before she decided what weight to give the reading.

She was honest with herself about it.

And then she decided the weight to give it anyway.

Some of them you may already know without realizing it.

She picked up her pen and opened the custodian notebook to a fresh page.

She wrote the sentence at the top of the page.

Then she drew a line under it and began to write her response, which she had been composing in the back of her mind since she sat down at the table. She addressed everything the family had written, confirming the Montana sealing from her perspective, adding details about the Carnegie Hall site that only someone who had been in the basement and found the inscription would know, describing the Ashcraft conversation and what the box had contained.

And at the end she added something she had not included in any previous correspondence.

She wrote about her father. Not by name. Just the fact of him. That she had recently discovered he might not have died when she was eight years old. That she had been following a thread through physical records and estate documentation that pointed toward someone who had been watching the seven sites for twenty years through a monitoring infrastructure she had found traces of in the databases before the grid went down. That she did not know where this person was or what exactly they had been doing or whether what she suspected about their identity was correct.

That she was not sure what she would do if it was correct.

She sealed the envelope and addressed it to the post office box on the letter she had received.

She did not know, as she walked to Gerald Sims's counter and added it to the outgoing stack, that on the other side of the world a man who had been reading her letters to the family for three weeks was about to read something that would require him to make a decision he had been postponing for twenty-three years.

She walked back to Carnegie Hall in the morning light and sat down at her east window table and opened her custodian notebook and looked at the sentence she had written at the top of the page.

Some of them you may already know without realizing it.

She looked at it for a long time.

Then she turned the page and went back to work.

CHAPTER 10: THE DAUGHTER

James spent the first day after the kitchen table conversation doing nothing that looked like preparation.

This was deliberate. Whatever surveillance the gang had established on the collaborator needed to see the same patterns it had been seeing. Same morning briefing attendance. Same perimeter check. Same evening presence at Carnegie Hall. Nothing that suggested the situation had changed, because the situation changing was the one thing that could not become visible before James was ready for it.

He attended the morning briefing and listened to Reeves's perimeter report and contributed two observations of his own and gave no indication that anything in his understanding of the situation had shifted overnight. He drove the farm circuit at dusk. He sat in the Carnegie Hall basement for two hours after the evening briefing reviewing the community resource inventory with Patricia Ashcraft.

He went home at ten and sat on his porch in the dark and thought about a daughter in an abandoned grain facility two miles off Benham Road, and then he went to bed.

On Day 2 he started building.

***

Without the tools he would normally have used, the process looked different than it would have looked six weeks ago. He could have run property records for every vacant or abandoned structure within a fifteen mile radius in twenty minutes, cross-referenced ownership against known associates, accessed the county's incident report database for the specific fingerprint that a group sheltering in an abandoned building left in a system that was paying attention.

None of that was available.

What was available was people.

He started with Reeves, who had twelve years of Dearborn County law enforcement behind him and the particular accumulated knowledge of a man who had responded to calls at most of the county's problem properties at one point or another. They sat in the Carnegie Hall basement with a county road map spread between them and Reeves talked while James marked.

Abandoned properties first. A former dairy operation on the ridge road north of the county line, vacant since the family sold the cattle three years ago. Two houses on the eastern township roads in estate disputes long enough that no one was maintaining them. A grain storage facility off Benham Road that a development company had bought and never developed, behind a chain link fence with a lock that Reeves said had been cut and replaced so many times over the years it was essentially decorative.

"The grain facility," James said. "You've been out there before."

"Twice," Reeves said. "Trespassing complaints, both times. Teenagers. Neither complaint went anywhere because by the time we got out there the teenagers were gone."

"Layout?"

"Main building is large. Steel construction on a concrete pad, built in the seventies. Sound structure despite the vacancy. Smaller outbuilding to the north, original farm equipment storage, and a working well somewhere on the property." Reeves looked at the map. "The access road comes off Benham Road about two miles east of the county road intersection. From Benham Road you can't see the facility at all. You'd have to know it was there."

James marked it and looked at the four properties he had marked and thought about logistics. A group holding someone needed water and shelter and enough distance from populated areas that noise was not a concern and enough road access that movement in and out was practical without being obvious.

The grain facility had all of it.

He thanked Reeves and went to find Danny McClanahan.

***

He found Danny at the post office dropping off the outgoing stack. Danny saw him coming and waited with the easy patience of someone who had learned that when James McClanahan was walking toward you with a specific quality of purpose it was worth waiting to find out why.

"The grain facility off Benham Road," James said. "You drive past that access road twice a day on the farm circuit."

"Yes," Danny said.

"Tell me what you've seen."

Danny worked through his mental record before he started talking. "Two weeks ago, maybe a little more, I noticed vehicle tracks on the access road. Passenger vehicles, not farm equipment. The tracks went in and came back out. I noticed because that road doesn't get used. In seven weeks of driving past it I had never seen fresh tracks on it before."

"How old were the tracks when you first saw them?"

"Two, three days. There had been a light rain the previous week and the tracks were in the dried mud from after the rain." He paused. "A week later I saw fresh tracks. Same vehicles by the width. They had been back."

"Anything else?"

"Last Thursday on the dusk run I smelled wood smoke from that direction. Not a campfire smell. Contained. Coming from inside a structure. Chimney smoke or a flue, and it was coming from the direction of that property."

"Before two weeks ago. Seven weeks of driving that road. Did you ever smell smoke from that property?"

"No," Danny said. "Never."

James nodded. "Keep driving the circuit. Don't change anything. Don't slow down when you pass that access road and don't look at it any longer than you look at anything else."

Danny looked at him. "You know where she is."

It was not a question. Danny had arrived at the conclusion through the particular intelligence of someone who had been paying close attention to everything happening in Moores Hill for seven weeks.

"Keep driving the circuit," James said again. "That's the most important thing you can do right now."

Danny nodded once and turned back toward the post office.

***

He went to Gary Whitfield in the afternoon.

Gary was in the yard splitting wood with the steady efficiency of someone who had decided that physical preparation was the most useful thing available in the hours when he was not on watch rotation. He set the maul down when James came through the gate and waited.

James told him what he had. The pieces Gary needed to help him think about the grain facility specifically.

Gary listened with his arms crossed, his eyes doing the thing that certain people's eyes did when processing operational information, assembling the picture.

"I know that facility," Gary said. "Played out there as a kid before the development company bought it. The main building has three windows on the south wall. They were boarded from the outside. If someone was inside they could get light through the gaps." He paused. "The north entrance opens onto a clear run to the outbuilding and the well. Someone who knew the property could move between those two points without being seen from the access road or Benham Road."

"How many ways in and out of the main building?" James said.

"Three. South entrance, which faces the access road. North entrance on the back side. And an emergency exit on the east wall, installed when the facility was operating, that opens outward." He looked at James. "The emergency exit hardware was rusted the last time I was out there. Fifteen years ago. From the inside you could push it open with enough force. From the outside you'd need something to work the mechanism and some motivation."

James thought about the layout. The south entrance visible from the road. The north entrance offering concealed movement between the building and the well. The emergency exit as a secondary option.

"The well," James said. "Good stone casing?"

"My grandfather helped dig it," Gary said. "That well is not going dry."

Water. Shelter. Concealed access between the two. A contained fire vented through whatever the building offered.

Everything a group needed to hold a location for weeks.

"I need you Thursday night," James said. "I need to observe the exchange and confirm the location before I build anything around it."

"I'll be there," Gary said.

James picked up one of the split pieces of wood from the pile and set it on the block and handed Gary the maul.

"Don't change your routine either," James said. "Nothing changes until Thursday."

Gary split the wood with a single clean stroke.

"Thursday," he said.

***

Thursday at dusk James was in position two hundred meters from the grain facility's main entrance.

He was in the tree line that ran along the northern edge of the property, lying flat on ground that was still warm from the day's heat, the particular warmth of June earth that had been absorbing sun since morning. The smell of it. Dry grass and soil and the faint mineral smell of the creek drainage that ran thirty meters to his left through the property's northern edge.

Gary was beside him, equally still, equally flat.

The tree line gave them a clear sight line to the area east of the south entrance where the exchange happened at a specific point marked by a piece of field stone, large enough to be found in low light, far enough from the building that the person making the exchange did not have to approach the entrance itself.

The light was doing what light did at this hour in June in southern Indiana. Going golden and then amber and then beginning its slow decline toward the gray that preceded full dark.

James watched the access road.

The collaborator arrived on foot at ten minutes before dusk, moving at the specific pace of someone who had made this walk enough times that the physical performance of it was automatic while the internal experience of it remained exactly what it had been the first time. James watched them cross from the access road to the exchange point and crouch at the field stone and leave the information packet and stand and wait.

Two minutes.

The south entrance opened.

One man came out. Moving with the unhurried confidence of someone operating in controlled territory. Thirties, heavyset, wearing clothing that had been functional before three weeks of hard use had reduced it. He crossed to the field stone without looking toward the tree line. Picked up the information packet. Opened it and looked at the contents the way James recognized as a professional check, not reading in detail but confirming what was there was what was expected.

He produced the photograph from his jacket pocket.

Set it on the field stone.

And went back inside.

Thirty seconds from the time he came out to the time the south entrance closed behind him.

James watched the collaborator pick up the photograph. Watched them stand for a moment with it in their hands, looking at it in the failing light, before putting it in their pocket and beginning the walk back to the access road.

He did not move until they were off the property.

Then he turned to Gary. "What you saw."

"One man," Gary said. "Which means either the others are inside with the girl or they're not there right now."

"They're inside," James said. "That exchange took thirty seconds and he came out alone. If the building wasn't occupied beyond him he would have taken longer. He's managing people in there and he came out and went back because the people in there needed managing."

Gary was quiet for a moment. "How many?"

"The night of the Miller farm incident, eight men in the field. Two got away. Six are in Reeves's custody. The man we just watched is not one of the eight. He's a different layer of the organization." James looked at the building. "So we don't know how many are inside."

"No," Gary said.

The last of the amber light was going out of the sky to the west. The tree line going dark faster than the open field to their right, the particular sequence of a rural Indiana dusk that James had been watching his whole life.

He thought about a daughter inside that building. Three weeks of it. The photographs with the handwritten dates. The particular psychological state of someone who had been held long enough that the holding had become its own kind of normal, who was waiting, without knowing what she was waiting for, for something to change.

He thought about what it would cost her if the change went wrong.

"I need four days," James said. "I need to build something that can do this correctly."

Gary looked at the facility.

"What does correctly look like?" Gary said.

"It looks like she comes home," James said. "Everything else is secondary to that."

Gary was quiet for a moment.

"Four days," he said. "Tell me what you need."

James stood up and brushed the ground from his clothes.

"People who can move quietly and who understand that the objective is the girl and nothing else. The east wall exit confirmed operable from the outside before we go in. And a way to know how many are in that building before we approach it."

"Danny can run the access road on the circuit," Gary said. "Count vehicles. Gives us a number to work with."

"Yes. Start tomorrow."

He turned and walked back through the tree line to the truck. Gary followed. The sounds of the evening settling around them, the crickets starting up, a bird somewhere in the tree line finishing its last business before dark.

There was work to do.

Four days.

He would not waste a single one of them.

CHAPTER 11: THE FIRE

Owen Mitchell had been cold for eleven days.

Not the manageable cold of a man who has chosen to be outside and who has the equipment to address it. The specific deep cold of someone who has been wet more days than dry and who has used most of his available energy staying warm enough to keep moving and has not had enough left over to get fully warm. The kind of cold that lived in the joints and behind the eyes and that no amount of moving generated enough heat to fully displace.

He had left Telluride six weeks ago in a rental car with a full tank of gas and the reasonable expectation that he would be home in two days. The grid failure abruptly changed those plans. The rental car had made it to western Kansas before the fuel situation made continuing in it impossible. He had traded the car for passage on a supply wagon heading east, which had gotten him as far as central Kansas before the wagon turned south toward Oklahoma and he had continued on foot.

The horse had come from a farm outside a town in eastern Kansas whose name he had written in his notebook and then lost the notebook somewhere in Missouri. A reasonable animal, not young, but sound enough for the road. It had carried him through the rest of Kansas and into Missouri and had died in a field in the western part of the state on a morning three weeks ago when he had woken to find it simply finished, the particular finality of an animal that had given everything it had and had nothing left.

He had sat with it for a while.

Then he had gotten up and walked east.

The mule he had acquired four days later in a small town in central Missouri, two days' walk from the Mississippi. Her name was

Margaret. He had named her after the first mile because she had the same quality of absolute unshakeable certainty about her own rightness that Margaret Hendricks had, the specific composure of a creature who had decided long ago that the world's opinion of her was largely irrelevant and who moved through that world accordingly.

She had cost him the last thing he had of any value.

Margaret the mule did not care about cold. She did not care about rain. She did not care about the particular quality of a man's misery or the depth of his exhaustion or whether the road ahead was longer than the road behind. She cared about moving forward at her own pace and stopping when she decided to stop and eating whatever was available and being left alone about all of it.

She was also worth more than anything else moving on these roads and Owen knew it. He had learned this quickly. A mule in the second month of a grid failure was transportation, hauling capacity, and a source of labor that nothing else available could match. He had seen the way people looked at Margaret when he passed through populated areas. He had adjusted his travel accordingly. He moved in the early morning and the late afternoon. He avoided large groups on the roads. He kept Margaret close at night and slept lightly.

He had found US 50 in central Missouri and had not left it.

Not the interstate. The interstates were where the desperate people moved, the ones caught far from home when the grid went down who had no plan and were following the largest road available on the theory that larger roads led somewhere useful. He had seen what the interstates looked like from a distance and had understood immediately that they were not safe for a man with a mule. Too many people. Too much desperation. Too many people who had already made the calculation that taking what someone else had was preferable to not having it.

US 50 was different.

It was the old road. The one that had existed before the interstates made it obsolete, running coast to coast across the country through towns that the interstate had bypassed and that had spent the past seventy years becoming quiet and forgotten. Most people moving in the current crisis did not know US 50 existed or did not think of it as going anywhere useful. A man who had spent years as an investigative reporter developing the specific habit of knowing things that most people did not know had thought of it immediately.

US 50 crossed the Mississippi at St. Louis and ran east through southern Illinois and into Indiana. It passed through Aurora, Indiana.

He had known about US 50 since he was a boy. Everyone raised in the Cincinnati tri-state area knew it the way they knew the back roads to their grandmother's house, not because they thought about it but because it was simply part of the geography of growing up there. Coast to coast. One of the old roads, the ones that existed before the interstates made them obsolete. It ran straight through Aurora Indiana. From Aurora north on SR 350 was twelve miles. Home.

He had not needed a map to know that. He had needed a dead horse and a mule named Margaret and the particular clarity that came from having nothing left to lose.

He knew exactly where he was going.

What he did not know was whether he had enough left to get there.

***

He found the creek in the late afternoon of the second day of the slow rain.

He had been looking for it, or for something like it, since the rain had started two days ago and had settled into the particular relentless gray quality of Midwestern spring rain that did not commit to being a real storm and did not relent into being merely damp but simply continued, hour after hour, with the patient indifference of weather that had no particular agenda and no particular schedule and was not going to be rushed by anyone's preference.

The creek ran along the south side of US 50 in the rolling country of central Missouri, between two fields that had been farmed until recently and were now simply fields in the particular way of agricultural land that has stopped being managed. There was a stand of cottonwoods along the bank, old ones with thick bark and wide canopies that made them useful as shelter in the imperfect but meaningful way of large trees.

He tied Margaret to a cottonwood away from the road where she could not be easily seen and stood in what passed for the shelter of the canopy and looked at the creek.

It was running clear over a gravel bed, cold and moving with the unhurried purpose of water that knew exactly where it was going and had been going there for longer than anyone alive could remember.

He looked at it for a moment.

Then he dug the fishing line and the single hook out of the bottom of his pack.

***

He had been carrying the fishing line since Kansas.

A man at a roadside camp outside of a small town had given it to him in exchange for nothing, simply pressed it into his hand when Owen mentioned he was heading east and asked if he had any food. Six feet of monofilament with a hook already tied to one end. Simple. Sufficient.

Owen had been saving it. The way you saved things when resources were genuinely finite and using them required being sure the use was worth it. He had passed creeks and small rivers along US 50 and had looked at them and had kept moving because the time it took to fish was time he was not moving east and moving east was the only job that mattered.

Today the rain had made the decision for him.

He dug through the pack for bait and found a piece of hardtack that had softened in the damp until it was the consistency of dough and pinched a small piece onto the hook and crouched at the edge of the creek and put the line in.

He waited.

The rain came down through the cottonwood canopy in the particular way of rain through large trees, not as drops but as a steady drip from the leaves above, cold and irregular, finding the back of his neck regardless of how he positioned himself.

Margaret stood at her cottonwood eating whatever she could reach and paid no attention to the rain whatsoever.

Twelve minutes.

The line went taut.

He pulled it in carefully with the particular focused patience of a man who understood that what was on the end of this line was not a fish. It was dinner. It was the difference between going to sleep with something in his stomach and going to sleep without.

It was a bluegill. Small. The kind of fish that a man with options threw back.

Owen looked at it.

He did not throw it back.

***

Getting a fire started was the work of forty minutes.

He had been using flint and steel since his lighter had run out of fuel in western Missouri, before the horse died, back when he had still been moving at a pace that felt like progress. The fire starter had come from the pack of a man who had made a poor decision about Margaret on a road outside of a small town and who had reconsidered after Owen made the specific case for reconsidering that a man made when he had nothing left to lose and the person in front of him had not yet understood that.

He had taken the fire starter and kept moving east on US 50.

Flint and steel required dry tinder and dry tinder required finding something the two days of slow rain had not reached, which meant digging under the leaf litter at the base of the cottonwoods and pulling out the compressed dry material that accumulated there protected from above by the canopy and from the sides by its own accumulated depth.

He built the tinder nest with the care of someone who understood that he had a limited number of strikes before the flint edge wore down enough to stop producing sparks reliably. He had been counting strikes since Kansas. He did not know exactly how many he had left. He knew it was not unlimited.

He struck.

The spark caught the tinder and he bent over it and breathed on it with the specific controlled breath of a man who had done this enough times to understand that breath was deliberate and measured and directed at exactly the right spot or it extinguished the thing it was meant to grow.

The tinder caught.

He fed it carefully. Small sticks first. The driest ones he had found under the leaf litter. Then slightly larger ones. The fire was not impressive. It was the size of a large man's cupped hands. But it was real and it was his and he had made it from nothing in the rain and that was enough.

He cleaned the bluegill with the economy of motion his grandfather had taught him on the banks of a reservoir outside Columbus when Owen was eight years old. Do the job. Do it correctly. Do not waste time doing it differently than it needs to be done.

He positioned the fish over the fire on a green stick cut from a young cottonwood branch.

He sat back on his heels and looked at it.

It was the first thing he had cooked over an actual fire in eleven days. The smell of it reached him even through the rain and he felt his stomach respond with the specific urgent attention of a body that has been operating on insufficient input for long enough that it has stopped pretending this is temporary.

He watched the fire.

He watched the fish.

The rain picked up.

Not all at once. In the gradual way that Midwestern rain increased, the drops coming faster and harder and the sound of it in the cottonwood canopy above changing from the intermittent drip of moderated rain to the continuous roar of real rain, rain with commitment, rain that had finally decided to be what it was going to be.

The fire went out.

Not dramatically. In the specific quiet way that fires went out when water fell on them, the hiss of it, the smoke rising briefly from the wet coals, and then nothing. The smell of extinguished fire. The smell of something that had been alive and was no longer alive.

Owen looked at the coals.

He looked at the raw fish on the green stick.

He looked at the rain coming through the cottonwood canopy above him.

He sat down in the mud beside the dead fire with the raw fish in his hand and something in him that had been held in place for a very long time let go.

***

He cried like a child.

Not with dignity. Not with the contained quality of a man allowing himself a measured emotional release. With the specific ungovernable quality of grief that had been managed and controlled and kept at a functional distance for too long and had finally found the moment when the management was no longer possible.

The raw fish. The dead fire. The rain. The mud. The mule that did not care.

It started there and went somewhere much larger very quickly and he did not try to stop it because he could not have stopped it and because some part of him that was older and wiser than the part that managed things understood that this was not weakness. This was the thing that had needed to happen for a long time and had been waiting for a moment when there was nothing left to hold it back.

He had traded the ring.

That was where it lived. Not in the fish or the fire or the rain or the mud or the eleven days of cold. In the ring. In the specific moment four days ago when he had stood in a field in central Missouri and looked at his hand and understood what the next step required and had taken it.

The ring was the wedding band Sarah Bennett had bought for him.

Not an engagement ring. A wedding band. She had bought it after he proposed, in the specific way of Sarah Bennett who did not wait for things to happen to her but moved toward them with the full confidence of someone who understood that life was what you decided it was going to be. She had put it in a drawer and told him she was ready when he was and she had laughed when she said it and the laugh had been completely genuine and he had understood in that moment that he was going to spend the rest of his life with this woman.

Mark Caldwell had made sure that did not happen.

Owen had been wearing the wedding band since the day they found her. Not as a statement. Not as a performance of grief for anyone else's benefit. Because taking it off required making a decision he was not capable of making and putting it on was the only thing that felt like the right response to something for which there was no right response.

You did not grieve Sarah Bennett the way you grieved someone who had been ill. There was no preparation. No slow arrival of the inevitable. There was Sarah on a Thursday and no Sarah on a

Friday and between those two facts a man named Mark Caldwell who had decided that what he wanted entitled him to take whatever he needed from whoever had it.

Mark Caldwell was dead now. In the ground where he belonged. That had not resolved anything. Grief did not resolve because the person responsible for it was dead. If anything the death of the man who had done it removed the last available object for the anger that lived alongside the grief, which left only the grief itself, without even the container of anger to give it a shape.

Owen had been carrying that for a long time.

The band on his finger had been the container for all of it. As long as it was there Sarah was not entirely gone. She was present in the object the way people were present in the things they had touched and chosen and given, and the band was all of those things, and as long as it was on his hand the particular future she had been reaching toward when Mark Caldwell ended her was not entirely foreclosed.

He had traded it for a mule.

He sat in the mud in Missouri in the rain and felt the full weight of that trade for the first time without the forward motion of the road to keep him from feeling it and he let it be as heavy as it was.

It was very heavy.

He did not try to make it lighter.

He stayed with it until it began to change.

***

Grief was strange.

Owen had known this in the abstract, the way you knew things about grief before you had experienced the specific version of it that would become yours. What he had not known, or had known and had refused to apply to himself, was that grief required moving through it rather than around it. That the management of it, the keeping it at a functional distance, was not the same as processing it. That you could carry something for years without it moving.

The band had been the mechanism that allowed the carrying without the moving.

As long as it was on his hand the grief had a container. Something that made its presence official and that told the world and told Owen himself that what had happened was real and had not been set aside or forgotten or moved past.

The band was gone.

He felt the grief move for the first time since Sarah Bennett was murdered.

Not resolve. Not end. Move. The specific quality of something shifting from the place it had been lodged into something with a different shape, less rigid, less fixed, still present but present differently, the way a river moved differently after a dam was removed, still water but water that was going somewhere now instead of being held in place.

He stayed with it until the rain began to ease.

***

It was full dark by the time he had rebuilt the fire.

The second attempt cost more strikes from the flint than he could comfortably afford. But he had done it and the fish was cooking and the small fire was real and warm in the specific way that earned warmth was warm, more than its actual temperature suggested.

He sat with his back against the cottonwood with his hands toward the fire and Margaret standing at her tree in the dark and thought about the road.

He was somewhere in central Missouri on US 50. The Mississippi crossing at St. Louis was two days ahead at Margaret's pace, maybe three in this rain. Then southern Illinois, flat and long, the kind of riding that would feel like it was never going to end and then would end. Then across Indiana. Then Aurora. Then SR 350 north.

Twelve miles.

He thought about Moores Hill.

He thought about James, who had been managing a crisis for however many weeks it had been now and who was doing it the way James managed everything, with a quiet competence that made it look simpler than it was. He thought about Emma, who had been working on something significant since before the outage and who was continuing to work on it through the outage with the specific focused patience that was her particular gift.

He thought about the diner.

He thought about Sarah McClanahan behind the counter with whatever she had rigged to keep the diner running and the community coming through her door every morning and Sarah feeding it the way she fed everything, without ceremony or expectation, because that was simply who she was.

He had been thinking about Sarah McClanahan for longer than he had been willing to admit to himself.

Not in the way he thought about Emma, who was his partner and his colleague and one of the people he trusted most in the world and who existed in a category that had never been anything other than what it was.

Differently.

In the specific way that you thought about someone when you were aware of their presence in a room before you registered them consciously. When you found reasons to be in places they were likely to be. When the particular quality of who they were was something you had been paying attention to without quite admitting you were paying attention to it.

He had not let himself get closer because the band was on his finger and the band meant something and getting closer to someone while it was on his finger felt like a betrayal of what it meant. He was not willing to do that to Sarah Bennett's memory or to Sarah McClanahan, who deserved someone who was fully present.

The band was gone.

He sat with that for a while. Not with guilt, or not only with guilt. With the specific quality of someone who has been waiting for permission they could not grant themselves and who has just had it granted by circumstances that left him no choice.

He did not know what Moores Hill looked like after months without power. He did not know what he was riding back into on a mule named Margaret with nothing to his name except the clothes on his back and the knowledge of how to start a fire with flint and steel in the rain.

What he knew was that he was going home.

And that for the first time since Sarah Bennett was murdered, home meant something it had not meant before.

He ate the fish.

It was the best thing he had tasted in weeks.

He put out the fire carefully and settled against the cottonwood with his coat pulled around him and listened to the creek and US 50 quiet in the dark beyond the tree line and Margaret doing whatever Margaret did in the dark which appeared to involve very little sleeping and a great deal of standing.

He would be in Indiana in five days.

He closed his eyes.

For the first time since Telluride, Owen Mitchell slept without dreaming of the road behind him.

He dreamed of the road ahead.

CHAPTER 12: THE LEGION

Mark Andres saw the scout coming from half a mile out.

Not because the scout was moving fast. Because of how he was moving. The specific urgency of someone carrying information they needed to deliver before it became too late to be useful, pushing through the July heat on a bicycle on the county road that ran parallel to I-74, his head down, his legs working with the focused economy of a man who had stopped thinking about anything except getting where he was going.

Mark was at his fence line when the scout reached him and stopped and put both feet on the ground and said: "Harrison."

Mark had been expecting something. Not Harrison. Harrison was two exits east of St. Leon on I-74, which meant whatever had happened there had happened close and recently enough that the information was still warm.

He listened. The scout talked for six minutes. Mark asked four questions. The answers were specific and they were bad and they were consistent with each other in the way that true things were consistent when you asked about them from different angles.

He thanked the scout and watched him continue west and stood at his fence line looking east toward the highway corridor and thinking about what thirty-six hours meant and what needed to happen inside those thirty-six hours.

Then he got in his truck and drove to find Karl Schuman.

***

Karl was splitting wood behind his house when Mark pulled in.

He was twenty-nine years old and had been home from his second tour for fourteen months. The outage had given his particular kind of attention somewhere useful to go and he had felt in the six weeks since the grid went down the specific uncomfortable relief of someone whose skills had found their context again.

He set the maul down when he saw Mark's face.

Mark told him. The group on I-74. The estimate of size, several hundred at minimum, the scout had observed them from distance and the word he used was army, not crowd, not mob, army, the specific word of someone who had seen organized movement and weapons and the deliberate momentum of people who had made decisions and were executing them. The horses and the mules. The wagons loaded with supplies and ammunition and the particular inventory of people who had been taking what they needed from every exit between Cincinnati and here and had gotten very good at it. What had happened at Harrison.

He did not describe what happened at Harrison in detail. He did not need to. The look on Mark's face when he said the word was sufficient.

Karl listened without interrupting. When Mark finished Karl looked east, the direction of the highway, for a long moment.

"How far back?" Karl said.

"Scout put them at maybe thirty-six hours," Mark said. "Moving steady. Not fast. They've got wagons and animals and they're not in a hurry because they haven't needed to be in a hurry."

Karl nodded. He thought about the exit ramp. About SR 1 running over I-74 on the overpass. About the geometry of it, the way the ramp curved up from the highway to the overpass road, the way the overpass itself sat above the interstate with a clear sight line down onto anything moving on the highway below.

He thought about East Central High School and the buses.

"I need runners," he said. "Dover, New Alsace, Yorkville. Everyone at the Legion tonight."

"I'll go to Dover," Mark said.

"Take someone with you," Karl said. "Go fast."

***

The American Legion hall in St. Leon sat off SR 46, less than a mile from the I-74 interchange, on a road that everyone in the surrounding communities knew the way they knew the roads to their own driveways. They had driven it for chicken dinners and wedding receptions and graduation parties for as long as anyone could remember. It had the particular quality of a building that had been made part of a community's identity through accumulated shared experience, through the ordinary occasions of ordinary life celebrated in its main hall under its particular light.

By seven that evening it held close to ninety people.

They came from St. Leon and Dover and New Alsace and Yorkville. The Bischoff family from St. Leon, three brothers and their father, arriving in two trucks. The Hiltz family from Dover. Bill Steinmetz from New Alsace, seventy-one years old, who sat in the second row with the composed patience of a man who had been through difficult things before. The Wilhelm family. The Kraus family. Beau Hornbach from Yorkville. The Zimmers from Dover, arriving with tools in the bed of their truck because someone in their household had already decided that tools were going to be needed.

Karl stood at the front where the head table was and looked at the faces of people he had known his whole life.

He told them what was coming. Clearly and completely and without softening it. The group on I-74. The estimate of size. The weapons. The horses and wagons. What had happened at Harrison.

When he finished the room was quiet.

Then he told them what he intended to do about it.

***

The Interstate 74 interchange at St. Leon had a specific geography that Karl had been thinking about since Mark pulled into his driveway.

Coming west on I-74, the exit ramp curved up and to the right, rising to meet SR 1 where it crossed over the highway on the overpass. The overpass sat above the interstate at elevation, the road surface of SR 1 looking down onto the highway below with the clear unobstructed sight line that elevated ground always provided to the people who held it.

The ramp was the only way up.

If you controlled SR 1 on the overpass, if you held that road surface and the approaches to it, anything coming up that ramp came up into whatever you had waiting for it at the top. There was no flanking route. There was no alternate approach. The ramp funneled everything that came off I-74 into a single narrow path that rose toward a road surface controlled by whoever got there first and stayed there.

Karl spread his hand-drawn diagram on the head table and the people in the room gathered around it.

"We don't meet them in St. Leon," he said. "We don't meet them at the four-way stop. We hold the overpass. Nothing comes off that ramp."

Beau Hornbach looked at the diagram. "The buses," he said.

"Yes," Karl said.

East Central High School sat on SR 46 within sight of the Legion, on the left side of the road as you came from the interchange. Its bus fleet was lined up in the lot where it had been sitting since the first week of the outage, when the school had closed and the buses had simply stopped running. Full-sized school buses. Heavy. Difficult to move without keys or fuel. Nearly impossible to move quickly under any circumstances.

Nearly impossible was not the same as impossible when you had two days and the right equipment and enough people who understood what the buses needed to do and why.

"We get the buses onto the overpass and across SR 1 before they reach the exit," Karl said. "Bumper to bumper across the road surface. They become the wall. We hold the wall from above and from the sides."

Bill Steinmetz looked at the diagram. "And below," he said. "Anyone on that ramp is below the overpass surface."

"Yes," Karl said.

The room understood what that meant. Karl watched it move through the faces, the specific understanding of people who were farmers and mechanics and parents and neighbors and who were now doing the mathematics of a defensive position and arriving at conclusions that none of them had expected to arrive at when they woke up that morning.

Carol Kraus, who had been a nurse for twenty-two years, said from the third row: "I'll need the Legion basement. Whatever happens out there I need to be set up before it starts."

"It's yours," Karl said.

"And I need people," she said. "Not fighters. People who can follow instructions under pressure and don't faint."

Three hands went up immediately. Two more after a moment. Carol looked at them and nodded.

***

They spent thirty-six hours building.

Getting the buses onto the overpass required fuel that the Zimmers had been storing in drums in their equipment shed and that they brought without being asked because they had understood what the buses were for the moment Karl mentioned them. It required drivers, four of them, running the buses one at a time from the East Central lot up SR 46 to the intersection with SR 1 and then west on SR 1 to the overpass and into position across the road surface. It required the Bischoff brothers and Beau Hornbach and six other men working through the night to push and align and chain the buses into a barrier that would hold against the specific pressure of several hundred people who had already demonstrated at Harrison that they were willing to apply significant force to things standing between them and what they wanted.

Karl was on the overpass at dawn both mornings.

The view from SR 1 looking down at I-74 was the view he had been thinking about since Mark pulled into his driveway. The highway surface below. The exit ramp curving up toward him. The specific geometric advantage of elevation, the way anything moving on the highway or the ramp was visible and exposed from above while the people on the overpass were not.

He walked the overpass surface both mornings looking at it the way he had been trained to look at ground. Where the positions were. What they covered. What they could not cover and what needed to cover those gaps. He made adjustments. He moved people. He had conversations with specific individuals about specific responsibilities that he needed them to understand before the moment arrived when there would be no time for conversation.

The scouts he had sent east came back on the second afternoon.

They had gotten close enough to observe and had observed for long enough to have a clear picture and what they reported confirmed and expanded what the traveler had told Mark Andres. Several hundred people. Horses and mules throughout, not the gentle farm animals of Dearborn County but animals that had been pushed and were showing it. Wagons loaded with the accumulated inventory of six exits worth of taking, food and fuel and tools and ammunition and the particular miscellany of desperate organized acquisition. Armed throughout. Not uniformly, not with military equipment, but with the specific variety of weapons that people accumulated when they had been taking them from every place they stopped.

The scout who had gotten closest said that the people at the front of the group had a quality he struggled to describe. He used the word gone. Not angry, he said. Not desperate the way desperate people looked when they still had something to lose. Gone. The look of people who had crossed a line somewhere back east and had kept walking after they crossed it until they were too far past it to see it anymore.

Karl thanked the scouts and told them to get food and rest and be back on the overpass before dawn.

***

They came on a Friday afternoon.

Karl was on the overpass when the first highway scout signaled from the tree line east of the interchange. He had positioned himself at the center of the bus line, the midpoint of the barrier across SR 1, where he could see both ends of it and both sides of the overpass and the ramp below and the highway in both directions.

He passed the signal down both sides of the line.

The positions settled into the specific quality of readiness that he recognized from the two times he had experienced it before, the held-breath quality of people who have prepared for something and are now waiting for it to arrive and have run out of things to do except be ready.

He looked down at the exit ramp.

They appeared on I-74 from the east in a column that stretched further back than he could see clearly in the afternoon light. The horses first, riders who were ranging ahead of the main body the way outriders ranged, assessing what was in front of them. Then the wagons. Then the mass of people on foot, hundreds of them, moving with the particular momentum of a group that had been moving together long enough that the movement itself had become the thing rather than the destination.

They slowed when they saw the interchange.

The riders at the front stopped and looked at the exit ramp and looked up at SR 1 on the overpass and Karl could see from his position the specific moment when they understood what they were looking at. The buses across the road. The people on the overpass above them. The geometry of the position.

One of the riders turned back toward the main body.

Karl watched the conversation happen below him, too far to hear, close enough to see the gestures and the specific quality of a decision being made by people who were weighing what they were looking at against what they had already done and deciding whether the calculation still worked.

It took four minutes.

Then the column started moving again and the riders turned back toward the ramp and Karl said to the people on either side of him: "Hold the line. Nothing comes off that ramp."

What followed he would not describe in detail to anyone afterward, not at the Legion that night and not in the weeks that followed. He would say that the overpass held. He would say that the position held. He would say that the specific advantage of elevation over a confined approach was exactly what his training had taught him it was and that the people of St. Leon and Dover and New Alsace and Yorkville had held their ground with the particular courage of people defending the specific ground they had grown up on and intended to grow old on.

He would say that the casualties on both sides were significant.

He would not say more than that.

What he carried privately, what he would be carrying for a long time, was the specific quality of what it looked like when several hundred people who had gone too far past a line to see it anymore encountered a position they could not break and had to make a decision about what came next. The specific human quality of that moment. The horses screaming on the ramp. The wagons blocking their own retreat. The sound of it.

He carried that.

The overpass held for four hours.

When it was over the column had turned back east on I-74, moving the way things moved when they had spent what they had and found nothing on the other side of it worth what it had cost. Not retreating in any military sense. Simply moving because staying was no longer an option and the next exit east was the direction that offered the possibility of something different.

Karl stood on the overpass in the long summer light and looked at the ramp below and the highway beyond it and felt the specific hollow exhaustion of someone who has been running at full capacity and has just been allowed to stop.

Mark Andres came and stood beside him.

They looked at the highway together without speaking for a long time.

"How many?" Mark said finally.

Karl looked at the ramp. At the highway. At the long empty interstate stretching east toward Harrison and the exits before it and the city at the end of it that had sent several hundred people west looking for what it no longer had.

"Too many on both sides," he said.

Mark nodded. He understood that was the answer Karl was going to give and that it was the only honest answer available and that it would have to be enough for now.

They walked back down SR 1 toward the Legion together.

***

The Legion infirmary was still running when they got back.

Carol Kraus was moving through it with the focused efficiency of someone who had not stopped since the position had been established and who was not going to stop until everyone who needed to be seen had been seen. Lizzie Zimmer and her family were there, as they had been throughout, feeding people with the quiet consistency of people who understood that the work of sustaining a community did not stop because the immediate crisis had passed.

Elsa Callahan was in the back of the main hall with the children, the ones who had been brought to the Legion because there was nowhere safer to leave them. She had kept them occupied and purposeful through the four hours on the overpass and she was still with them now, talking to them in the low steady voice of someone who understood that what children needed after something frightening was the continued presence of an adult who was not afraid.

Karl looked at the hall. At the people in it. At the folding tables and the chairs and the particular quality of a place that had been a wedding reception venue and a chicken dinner hall and a graduation party space and was now something else, would be something else in the memory of everyone who had been in it for the past thirty-six hours, while also somehow still being what it had always been.

He sat down at one of the tables.

Lizzie Zimmer put a plate in front of him without a word.

He ate.

Outside, on I-74, the summer evening went about its business. The highway that had carried millions of people back and forth across the Midwest for decades sat quiet in the fading light. Empty in the way that things were empty when the conditions that made them useful had changed.

The citizens of St Leon, Dover, New Alsace and Yorkville, joined together, well over a thousand strong, and stopped a hostile takeover or their communities.

Twelve miles to the southwest, Moores Hill did not yet know what had happened at the St. Leon interchange.

It would know soon enough.

CHAPTER 13: THE EXECUTOR'S RECORDS

The box arrived on a Tuesday morning in the fifth week.

Gerald Sims had it behind the counter when Emma came in for the regular mail check, a medium-sized cardboard box with her Carnegie Hall address written in the careful block letters of someone who had been sending professional correspondence for forty years and had not changed the habit in retirement. The return address was the Montgomery Road address in Cincinnati. Franklin Marsh, Attorney at Law, Retired.

Gerald looked at it with the expression he reserved for items that fell outside the normal parameters of personal correspondence. "Heavier than a letter," he said.

"Yes," Emma said.

She carried it to Carnegie Hall under her arm with Rufus beside her and set it on her east window table without opening it. The morning briefing was in twenty minutes and she wanted to attend before she sat down with whatever Marsh had sent, because James had indicated the previous evening that he had information from the shortwave that the community needed to hear.

She went downstairs.

***

The briefing room was fuller than usual.

Word had traveled, the way word traveled in Moores Hill, through the particular informal communication network of a small town that had been operating without electronic communication for five weeks and had developed, in the absence of it, something older and more personal. People told each other things. They told their neighbors and their neighbors told the people they saw at the post office and the people at the post office told the people at Margaret Hendricks's information table, and by the time the morning briefing began the room held close to sixty people instead of the usual thirty.

James stood at the front without his notebook.

Emma noticed that immediately. James always had his notebook at the morning briefings, the small leather-covered one he carried in his shirt pocket and consulted for specific numbers and dates. The absence of it meant what he was about to say had not been written down. Which meant either it had arrived too recently to write down or he had decided it should not be written down yet.

He waited until the room settled.

"I have two things to tell you," he said. "I'm going to tell you both of them directly and I'm going to ask you to sit with what you hear before you respond, because both of them require a clear head and neither of them changes what we do today."

The room was already quiet. It got quieter

"There was an incident on Interstate 74 yesterday. A large group, estimates range from several hundred to over a thousand people, moving east to west along the highway corridor out of Cincinnati. Not an organized group. A mob, in the honest sense of the word, people who had been without food and without resources long enough that individual decision making had given way to collective movement in whatever direction seemed to offer something."

He paused.

"The group encountered resistance at the St. Leon interchange. Residents of St. Leon and people from the surrounding communities, Dover, New Alsace, Yorkville, who had organized in the days before the encounter after receiving warning from travelers. The confrontation lasted several hours. The defenders held the interchange. The mob did not get through."

He stopped again.

"The casualty count on both sides was significant. The estimates I have are not reliable enough to give you a specific number. What I can tell you with confidence is that it was the kind of engagement that leaves a mark on every community that hears about it. And I'm telling you about it because US 350 runs through the center of this town, and the people who organized at St. Leon had warning, and the warning is what made the difference."

The room was very still.

Emma watched the faces. The particular quality of sixty people receiving information that reorganized their understanding of what they were inside of. Five weeks ago the outage had been an emergency. Three weeks ago it had been a sustained crisis. What James had just described was something with a different name that none of them had been ready to apply yet.

"What does this mean for us?" Tom Hargrove said. His voice was steady. He was doing the arithmetic the way he always did.

"It means the watch on US 350 becomes the priority it should have been from the beginning," James said. "And it means the community needs to have a conversation about what we do if what happened at St. Leon moves in our direction. That conversation needs to happen today. I'd like to have it this afternoon at Carnegie Hall. Everyone who can come should come."

He looked at the room.

"The second thing." He said it without preamble, the way he said things that were worse than the thing that had come before them and that he was not going to soften by building toward them slowly. "This came through last night. A chemical facility in Evansville lost containment approximately two weeks into the outage. The specific facility has not been confirmed through the sources available to me. What has been confirmed is that the failure produced a fire that burned for six days and that the smoke and chemical dispersal from that fire affected a significant portion of the city."

The room had been still before. It was a different kind of still now.

"Casualty estimates are not reliable," James said. "What the shortwave operators are reporting is that the southern and central portions of Evansville sustained the most significant impact. Emergency services were overwhelmed within the first hours." He paused. "The University of Evansville campus is in the southern portion of the city."

Emma heard that sentence and felt something move through her that took her a moment to identify.

She knew what the University of Evansville was. She knew its relationship to Moores Hill College, the institution that Robert Moore had founded in 1854, that had operated in Carnegie Hall for decades before closing and eventually finding its way, in a different form, to Evansville. She knew that the building Robert Moore had built still stood in Moores Hill because her mother had protected it and Patricia Ashcraft had cast a deciding vote. She knew that the institution itself, the academic legacy, the living continuation of what Moore had created, had been in Evansville.

Had been.

She looked at Carnegie Hall's stone walls. At the building that had survived everything because the right people had made the right decisions at the right moments. The only surviving piece of what Robert Moore had built. Not the institution. Not the legacy. The building. The chamber underneath it. The ash circles. The knowledge that Emma was carrying forward into a future that Robert Moore had not lived to see.

James let the room sit with it for a moment. Then he said: "I'm telling you this because you need to know what is happening outside this community. Not to frighten you. To help you understand what Moores Hill is inside of." He looked at the faces in the room. "What we have built here in five weeks is not ordinary. I want you to understand that. What happened in St. Leon and what happened in Evansville is the context for what we have done here. Remember that when the work feels hard."

He closed the briefing.

***

Emma went upstairs and sat at her east window table and looked at the box from Franklin Marsh for a long time without opening it.

Outside the east windows Main Street was going about its morning with the adapted rhythm of a community that had been doing this for five weeks and had found its stride. People moving with purpose. The particular economy of motion that developed when people stopped doing things out of habit and started doing them out of necessity. It looked like competence. It looked like what James had described in the briefing room. It looked, from the outside, like something that had been built intentionally.

She thought about the University of Evansville. About the specific quality of an institution being erased from the world. About what it meant that the only surviving piece of what Robert Moore had built was the building she was sitting in, and the knowledge she was carrying, and the network she was rebuilding from the ash circles up.

Rufus put his chin on her foot.

She opened the box.

***

Marsh had included a note on top. Handwritten, brief, in the same careful professional script as the address on the outside.

Miss Caldwell, he had written. I found these in storage after your visit. I have been keeping them longer than I am required to because something in my professional judgment told me they were the kind of records whose value was not yet apparent. I believe their value is apparent now. I hope they are useful to you. I am sorry I cannot tell you more than they contain. FM.

She set the note aside.

The original Caldwell estate file lay beneath it. Not a copy. The original, with the specific physical texture of documents that had been handled repeatedly over twenty-three years, the slight softening of the paper at the edges, the corners of the pages worn to a gentle curve from being lifted and set down and lifted again. The ink had the quality that ink acquired with age and light exposure, slightly faded at the margins, darker where the pen had pressed harder at the beginnings of sentences. Marsh had kept it the way he kept things, with the professional thoroughness of someone who believed that records outlasted the immediate purposes they were created to serve.

She lifted the first page and felt the weight of it.

Real documents had a physical presence that reproductions did not carry. She had been working with reproductions at the county historical society, good reproductions, clear and complete, but reproductions nonetheless. What she was holding now were the actual pages that Franklin Marsh had handled in 2002 while he was noticing that something was wrong and deciding what to do about the noticing. His fingerprints, long faded, were on these pages. His professional unease was in the careful organization of them, the way he had ordered and reordered the documents in the file in the particular sequence of someone who kept returning to a question they could not answer and hoping that a different arrangement would reveal something new.

She went through it with the same discipline she brought to everything in the historical society archive.

Not looking for what was there. Looking for what was not there.

The first absence was on page twelve. The financial disclosure that should have accompanied a death certificate filing of this type, the accounting of assets held at the time of death that the estate process required before distribution could begin. It was not there. In its place was a notation in Marsh's handwriting, a single line, the kind of placeholder that attorneys used when a document was expected but had not yet arrived. The document had never arrived. The placeholder was still there, twenty-three years later, marking the space where something should have been.

She documented it in her custodian notebook. Page twelve. Financial disclosure. Absent.

The second absence was on page twenty-seven. A property transfer record for a piece of land in Dearborn County that appeared in the estate inventory but whose transfer documentation was not in the file. The inventory listed it. The corresponding paperwork that should have accompanied the transfer was not present. Another Marsh notation in the margin, smaller this time, in the handwriting of someone who had noted an absence and then noted it again later and then stopped noting it because it had become clear that the documentation was not going to appear.

Page twenty-seven. Property transfer documentation. Absent.

She turned pages. Reading carefully. Not rushing. The morning light moved through the east windows at the angle she had been working by for five weeks, the familiar quality of it something she had stopped noticing the way you stopped noticing familiar things, which meant she only noticed it now when she looked up from the file and felt the particular quality of the light on her hands and on the pages and understood that she had been sitting here for two hours.

She kept reading.

The third absence was the one that mattered most. She found it on page thirty-eight, or rather she found the place where it should have been on page thirty-eight and was not. The witness attestation for the will itself. In an estate of this size and complexity, the will required two witness signatures at the time of execution and those witnesses were required to provide attestations confirming that they had been present and that the testator had been of sound mind and had signed of their own free will. One attestation was present. The second was not.

An estate could not be legally administered without both attestations. The absence of one should have stopped the process. It had not stopped the process. The process had continued and concluded and the estate had been administered and closed despite the absence of a document that should have made the closing legally impossible.

Someone with significant authority over the filing process had allowed it to close anyway.

She documented it. Page thirty-eight. Second witness attestation. Absent.

Three absences. Each one individually the kind of thing that might be attributed to administrative oversight in a complex estate. Together they described something else. Together they described a file that had been shaped. Not falsified, nothing in the file was false in any verifiable sense, but shaped, the way water shapes itself to the container it's in, the contents arranged to produce a specific impression while the absence of certain things ensured that the impression could not be fully examined.

She sat back and looked at what she had documented.

Then she went looking for what was present that should not have been.

This was a different kind of search and she had learned, through months of investigative work, that it required a different quality of attention. Absence announced itself through the gaps it left in expected patterns. Presence of something anomalous did not announce itself at all. Anomalous things sat in the middle of ordinary things and looked ordinary until you had been looking long enough that the ordinary things became transparent and what was underneath them became visible.

She turned pages slowly. Reading the ordinary things. Letting them become transparent.

She found it on page forty-one.

A single line in a correspondence summary. The kind of notation that attorneys made in working files to track communications without transcribing them in full, the professional shorthand of someone managing multiple matters simultaneously. A call received. A date. A duration of fifteen minutes. And a name.

Not Robert Caldwell's name.

A man's name she did not recognize, with a Cincinnati area code beside it, dated three weeks before the reported date of Robert Caldwell's death on the interstate outside Columbus.

She looked at that line for a long time.

She looked at it the way she looked at things that required the full quality of her attention, which was completely and from every angle and without the interference of what she wanted it to mean. She looked at it as data. A call received. A specific date. A name she did not recognize. Fifteen minutes.

Someone had called Franklin Marsh three weeks before Robert Caldwell's reported death.

Not Robert Caldwell. The name was not Robert Caldwell and was not a name that appeared anywhere else in the estate file, not as a family member, not as a financial institution, not as a property holder or a legal representative or any of the parties whose names normally populated an estate proceeding of this type.

Someone whose name appeared in the working file and nowhere else.

Someone who had called Marsh three weeks before the death and had spoken to him for fifteen minutes and whose name Marsh had recorded in his working file with the reflexive thoroughness of a man who recorded everything and had not, perhaps, fully understood at the time what he was recording.

Someone who had known, three weeks before Robert Caldwell's reported death, that there was going to be an estate to administer.

Emma wrote the name in her custodian notebook and underlined it once.

She looked at what she had.

Three absences that required deliberate construction to produce. One presence that required foreknowledge to explain. And a name that was not Robert Caldwell's but that was connected to the estate before the estate should have existed.

She thought about her father. About the financial accounts Gerald Forsythe had described, registered under a name that was not Robert Caldwell. She had not yet found the connection between those accounts and the name in Marsh's working file.

She thought that she was about to find it.

She wrote three questions in her custodian notebook beneath the name and looked at them.

Who are you.

How did you know.

Where did the money come from.

Outside the east windows Main Street continued its afternoon. The community that James had described in the briefing room, the thing that had been built here in five weeks, went about the work of surviving with the quiet competence of people who had made a decision about what they were and were living inside that decision every day.

She thought about St. Leon. About the casualty count that James had not been able to give them a number for because the number was too large to be reliable. About what it meant that the warning had been the difference.

She thought about the University of Evansville and about the stone walls around her and about what the stone walls contained and what they had contained for over a hundred years without anyone knowing exactly what they were containing or why it mattered.

She knew why it mattered.

She closed her notebook and opened it again to the page with the three questions and looked at them for a moment. Then she picked up her pen and began, in the careful methodical way she began everything that required methodical care, to plan how she was going to answer them.

The thread was real. It was in her hands. She was not going to lose it.

***

She had been counting days for two weeks by marking the concrete floor with a stone she had found in the corner of the space on the third day.

Fourteen marks now. Small ones, carefully spaced, in a row along the base of the metal wall where they would not be easily seen. She did not know why it mattered that they not be seen. It just felt important to have something that was only hers.

The food had stayed consistent. Twice a day. Not enough but enough. She had started doing exercises in the space, the ones from gym class, not because she felt like exercising but because the physical therapist who had come to her school last year to talk about mental health had said that the body and the mind were connected and that moving the body changed the chemistry of the mind and she had thought that was the kind of thing adults said when they did not have anything more useful to say but she had decided two weeks into a concrete room with no windows to try it anyway.

It helped. Not a lot. Some.

She had stopped being afraid in the way she had been afraid in the first days. The fear had changed into something different, not gone but transformed into a specific quiet watchfulness that she recognized as more useful than the original fear. The original fear was reactive. This was something else. This was the thing that happened when you had been afraid for long enough that the fear became the baseline condition and you had to find a way to function inside it.

She was functioning inside it.

She thought about school sometimes. Not with longing exactly. With the specific quality of someone cataloguing the contents of a life that existed somewhere outside the concrete room and that she was keeping carefully in her memory the way you kept something valuable in a place you could find it again.

Her locker combination. The way the cafeteria smelled on pizza day. The particular creak of the third step on the staircase to the second floor that everyone knew about and stepped over automatically.

She kept these things in careful order.

She added one more mark to the row along the base of the wall.

Fourteen days.

She did not know how many more there would be.

She put the stone back in its corner and did her exercises and waited for the afternoon feeding and paid attention to the sounds of the facility around her and held the contents of her life carefully in her memory against the day she would need them again.

She was going to need them again.

She had decided that on the first night and she had not undecided it since.

CHAPTER 14: THE PROOF OF LIFE

The four days between the kitchen table and the Thursday exchange were the most disciplined of James's life.

Not physically. He had been through physical disciplines that made four days of community management look straightforward. Mentally. The discipline of knowing something specific and urgent and actionable and choosing, deliberately, to act on none of it until the moment was right. The discipline of sitting in briefings and walking the perimeter and driving the farm circuit and attending every community obligation while carrying, underneath all of it, the knowledge of a daughter in an abandoned grain facility two miles off Benham Road and a plan that was still being assembled and that could not be rushed without becoming a plan that failed.

He talked to every veteran in Moores Hill who had infantry or special operations experience. Not all at once. One at a time, in conversations that he framed as general preparedness discussion until he had enough of a read on each person to tell them what the conversation was actually about. He needed people who understood that the objective was the girl and that everything else, every other consideration, was secondary to the girl coming home.

He found four of them.

Gary Whitfield first, who had been in from the beginning and who James trusted with a completeness he trusted very few people. They sat at Gary's kitchen table on the evening of Day 1 and James laid it out plainly, the facility, the girl, the dead drop system, what Thursday required. Gary listened without expression until James finished. Then he said: what do you need from me between now and then. Not whether he was in. Whether he was in had apparently been decided before James finished the first sentence.

A former Marine named Len Doss who had been running a landscaping business for eight years and who listened to James's description of the situation with the focused quiet of someone whose training was still entirely present in him despite the years of civilian distance. Len had the particular physical stillness of people who had learned that stillness was its own kind of readiness. He asked three questions when James finished. Each one was the right question. James answered all three and Len said he would be at Gary's house at two-thirty Thursday morning.

A woman named Carol Beatty who had done two tours as a combat medic and who, when James explained what the operation required, said she was in before he finished the sentence and then asked whether there was a medical situation developing at the facility that he knew about because if there was she needed different equipment than if there wasn't. James said he didn't know. Carol said then she would prepare for both. She spent the following morning going through her medical kit at her kitchen table with the systematic thoroughness of someone who had been doing this for years and who understood that the difference between a kit that saved a life and one that didn't was often a single item that hadn't been packed because someone had assumed it wouldn't be needed.

The fourth was Danny McClanahan, who James had not initially considered because Danny's value was in his knowledge of the roads and the farm circuit and the particular intelligence that came from moving through the same ground twice a day for seven weeks. But Danny had come to James on Day 2 of the preparation period and had said, without preamble, that he had done three years in the Army before coming home and that he understood what was happening and that he wanted to be part of it.

James looked at him for a moment.

"You drive the circuit," he said. "On every pass of the grain facility access road between now and Thursday, you count vehicles on or near that property. Anything you can see from the road without slowing down. Same speed, same rhythm. Nothing changes."

"And Thursday night?" Danny said.

"Thursday night you're my driver," James said. "You know those roads better than anyone. If something goes wrong and we need to move fast, I need someone who knows exactly where they're going in the dark without headlights."

Danny nodded once. It was enough.

***

He talked to Reeves on the morning of Day 3.

Not about the operation specifically. About resources. What Reeves had available in terms of restraints, medical supplies, and the two officers who had been on rotation since the beginning of the outage and who Reeves trusted to follow specific instructions under pressure. He framed it as contingency planning for the community watch escalation, which was not entirely untrue, and Reeves listened and provided what James asked for and did not ask the questions he clearly understood James was not ready to answer yet.

At the end of the conversation Reeves looked at him steadily.

"When you're ready to tell me what this is," Reeves said, "I'm ready to hear it."

"Thursday night," James said. "After."

Reeves nodded. He had been in law enforcement long enough to understand that there were situations where the sequence of information mattered and that asking for it out of sequence could compromise the situation. He went back to the perimeter report he had been working on.

***

Carol Beatty walked the approach with James on the afternoon of Day 3.

Not close. A farm road that ran parallel to the property's northern edge, far enough from the facility that they were not visible from the building but close enough that Carol could get a physical sense of the ground between the farm road and the east wall exit. She moved through the field at the edge of the farm road with the practical attention of a medic assessing a route, noting the footing, the sight lines, the distance.

"Forty meters from the exit to the tree line," she said. "On open ground."

"Yes," James said.

"Condition of the subject unknown."

"Unknown," James said. "Photographs show her mobile. Three weeks of captivity with uncertain food and water access."

Carol looked at the ground between the farm road and the distant facility wall. She was doing the calculation that James had already done, the one that produced an answer that was workable but not comfortable. Forty meters of open ground with a subject who might be able to run or might need to be supported. In the dark. With whatever was happening inside the building still resolving behind them.

"I'll be at the exit when you bring her out," Carol said. "Not inside. I need to be positioned at the exit so I can assess her the moment she's through the door and start moving her toward the truck without losing time."

"Agreed," James said.

"And James," Carol said. She looked at him with the directness she brought to everything. "If she's in worse shape than the photographs suggest, we are not stopping to manage it in the field. We get her in the truck and I manage it while Danny drives. Clear?"

"Clear," James said.

They walked back to the farm road. The facility sat behind its tree line in the afternoon light, looking exactly like what it was, an abandoned building in a rural county that nobody had found a use for. Nothing about it from the outside suggested what was inside it.

That was the point.

***

Danny's vehicle counts came in on Day 3 and Day 4.

Two vehicles on Day 3, both visible from the road on the approach to the access road turnoff, parked in the screening provided by the facility's perimeter fence. A third vehicle on Day 4 that had not been visible on the Day 3 pass, either arrived between circuits or parked in a position the earlier angle hadn't revealed.

Three vehicles. James looked at that number and thought about what it suggested in terms of personnel. Not a scientific calculation. An informed estimate based on experience and the operational logic of a group that had been running a sustained operation for three weeks and that had sent eight people to the Miller farm and had two escape and had four in Reeves's improvised custody. The math of the organization was not fully visible to him. What was visible was three vehicles at a facility that was housing at minimum one hostage and the man who had conducted the dead drop exchange and whatever additional personnel the organization had committed to maintaining the location.

He had four people going in.

He thought about that ratio for a long time and came to the same conclusion he always came to when the numbers were not in his favor. Numbers mattered less than surprise. Surprise mattered less than clarity of objective. A team of four people with total clarity of objective and the element of surprise had significant advantages over a larger group that was not expecting them and was not organized around a specific defensive purpose.

He had been in situations with worse ratios.

He had come home from all of them.

He went to sleep on Wednesday night with the plan assembled in his head in the complete and specific way that plans needed to be assembled before they were executed, every contingency addressed, every role clear, every sequence understood by every person who was part of it. The particular quality of pre-operational calm that he had learned to recognize in himself over the years, not the absence of awareness but the product of having done everything that could be done before the thing itself.

***

Thursday arrived with the quality of a day that did not know it was significant.

The morning briefing. The farm circuit report from the overnight. The community resource update from Tom Hargrove. The postal situation from Gerald Sims. A question from Earl Hendricks about the diesel supply for the farm generators that James answered with the specific numbers Reeves had given him two days ago. The ordinary administrative work of a community managing its fifth week without power, moving through its adapted routines with the efficiency of people who had stopped expecting the situation to resolve and had started building their lives inside its continuation.

James moved through all of it with the same presence he brought to every briefing and every conversation, giving each thing the full attention it deserved, storing nothing away for later that needed to be handled now. He had learned that the way to manage a day that ended with a significant operation was to make the day as ordinary as possible until the moment it stopped being ordinary. Anticipation was energy spent before the moment that needed it.

He did not anticipate.

He drove the perimeter circuit at dusk the way he drove it every evening. The farms in the June light, the cattle at the fence lines, the particular quality of the landscape going from day to evening at this latitude in this season with the long slow unhurried quality of a place that had been making this same transition every evening for a very long time. He stopped at the Kowalski place and talked to Steve about the rebuilt smokehouse and the status of the preserved pork and whether the community distribution schedule was meeting the farm family's needs. He drove past the Henderson farm and waved to Paul Henderson on his porch.

He drove past the grain facility access road without slowing.

Two vehicles visible through the fence line screening. The same two that had been there for two days. The third was not visible from this angle, which meant it was either still parked in the position the Day 4 pass had found it or had left the property. He filed the observation and kept driving.

He was back at Carnegie Hall by eight-thirty. He sat in the basement for an hour working on the community resource inventory the way he worked on it every evening, in the quiet methodical way that made the work look like what it always looked like, which was a man doing the work that needed doing.

At nine-thirty he went home and slept for four hours.

***

He was at Gary's house at two in the morning.

The four of them in Gary's kitchen in the dark with a battery lantern on the table between them. James went through it once. The layout. The approach. The entry sequence. The positions. The extraction path. Each person's role from the moment the truck stopped on the farm road to the moment the truck left it.

He went through it once and then he stopped.

He looked at each of them.

Gary had the specific settled quality that James associated with people who had done this kind of work before and who approached the execution of it with the particular respect owed to things that required being done correctly. Len Doss had his arms crossed and his eyes slightly unfocused, running the sequence internally, checking it against his own experience. Carol had her kit in her lap, closed, her hands resting on top of it with the composed patience of someone who had been here before and who understood that the waiting was its own kind of work.

Danny was looking at James.

"The objective is the girl," James said. "Everything else is secondary. If at any point the operation requires us to abandon any other objective to protect her, we abandon it without discussion. Questions?"

No questions.

"We move in ten minutes," James said.

***

The approach to the grain facility at three in the morning was the quietest James had been in five weeks.

Not quiet in the sense of absence of sound. The June night was full of its own sounds, crickets and frogs and the particular ambient life of a rural Indiana night that had nothing to do with human concerns. Quiet in the specific internal sense of someone moving toward a thing they have prepared for completely and are ready for completely and have committed to without reservation.

Danny stopped the truck on the farm road behind the property with the engine off and the lights off and they sat for sixty seconds letting their eyes adjust and their ears calibrate to the sounds of the place.

James listened.

The facility. The sounds coming from inside it, faint but present, the sounds of an enclosed space that was occupied. A voice at the far end of the building, too distant to make out words, the specific quality of someone talking to pass time rather than to communicate anything specific. A door somewhere on the interior. The chain link fence section at the northern edge of the property moving in the light air.

Four people inside. Maybe more. He would know in a few minutes.

He signaled Gary.

Gary and Len moved to the east wall first with the tool Gary had collected from Tom Hargrove's back room two days ago and the oiled hinges that Carol had identified as a requirement and that Gary had addressed during the afternoon walkthrough. They worked the emergency exit mechanism in the dark with the patience of people who had been briefed precisely on what they were doing and were doing it precisely as briefed.

Fifty seconds.

The door opened outward without sound.

James looked at Carol, positioned at the exit as they had planned, her kit open and her attention already oriented toward the interior. She gave him a single nod.

He went through first.

***

The interior of the main building was lit by two lanterns positioned near the center of the large space, their warm light casting the interior into illuminated middle and shadowed edges. James stood inside the east exit with his back against the wall and let his eyes adjust and used the three seconds of adjustment to take in everything the light showed him.

Four people visible. Three men grouped near the lanterns in the posture of people who had been awake too long and were managing it with the collapsed patience of exhaustion. A fourth at the south entrance in a watch position, standing but with the diminished alertness of three in the morning when the body's insistence on sleep was hardest to override.

He signaled Gary and Len. Gary moved along the west wall in the shadow toward the watch position at the south entrance, moving with the unhurried controlled pace of someone who understood that speed at the wrong moment was worse than patience. Len moved in the opposite direction toward the three men near the lanterns.

James moved toward the north end of the building.

The partitioned section Gary had described was there, a wood-framed interior wall that had been the facility's original office space, its door standing half open. He went through it.

A sleeping bag on the concrete floor. A lantern turned low. A young girl, asleep, her face in the low light carrying the specific vulnerability of someone whose body had taken sleep because it needed sleep regardless of the circumstances, her breathing the slow regular breathing of genuine exhaustion rather than performed calm.

She was thin. Three weeks of inadequate food had produced the specific thinness that settled around the face and the wrists and the collarbone, the places where weight left first. But she was breathing and she was uninjured in the visible sense and she was here and that was the thing that mattered.

James crouched beside her and put his hand gently on her shoulder.

She woke the way people woke who had learned over three weeks that waking could mean anything, with a sharp intake of breath and the full-body alertness of someone whose nervous system had been on continuous threat assessment for an extended period. Her eyes found him in the low light and he watched the assessment happen in real time, the rapid reading of an unfamiliar face in an unfamiliar position, the particular held moment before the response.

He said her name quietly.

He said his name. He said he was the deputy from Moores Hill. He said her parents had sent him and that she was going home.

He watched her face receive that information.

There was a moment, just a moment, when she looked at him with the expression of someone who has been told something they want desperately to believe and who is deciding whether to believe it. He held her gaze steadily and waited.

She believed it.

From the other end of the building he heard Gary's voice, steady and calm, giving instructions. Then Len's. The sounds of a situation being resolved through the application of clear authority and the overwhelming advantage of surprise, which was the cleanest possible resolution and the one he had planned for.

He helped her to her feet. She was unsteady, the specific unsteadiness of someone whose body had been operating in a constrained space for three weeks and was relearning what standing fully upright felt like.

"Can you walk?" he said.

She said yes.

He took her through the partitioned door and back across the main building floor, past the lanterns and the three men now face down on the concrete with Len standing over them with the patient unhurried authority of someone who had done this before and understood that calm was the most powerful thing in the room.

Gary was at the south entrance. He looked at James as they passed and gave a small nod.

James took her through the east exit into the June night.

Carol was there. Carol put her hands on the girl's arms with the immediate professional focus of someone assessing a patient and said her name and said she was a medic and that they were going to walk to the truck together right now. She asked two questions while they walked, specific clinical questions delivered in a calm matter-of-fact tone that was designed to get useful information without introducing alarm, and she listened to the answers and nodded and kept walking.

Forty meters of open ground to the tree line.

Danny had the truck running with the lights off. He looked at James across the roof of the truck as they came through the tree line and James gave him a single nod and Danny got in and started moving before the doors were fully closed, the truck rolling out through the farm road and onto the county road with the lights still off, moving through the rural Indiana dark at three in the morning with Carol Beatty in the back seat doing the work she had come to do.

Eleven minutes from entry to the county road.

James sat in the passenger seat and watched the dark fields moving past the window and thought about a parent sitting in a house on the edge of Moores Hill who did not yet know that their daughter was eleven minutes away.

He thought about the kitchen table and what had been set down on it three days ago. The weight of it. The particular courage of someone who had been carrying something alone for three weeks and had finally put it down and trusted him with it.

He had not let that trust go to waste.

Danny drove through the dark without headlights for another mile and then turned them on and the road ahead came into view, the familiar county road running toward Moores Hill in the early morning, and James watched it come and felt the particular exhausted satisfaction of someone who had done the right thing in exactly the right way and who understood, with the honesty he brought to everything, that it had gone right because four people had been ready and the plan had been sound and the girl had been where he believed she would be.

He would take that.

There was always more work to do.

Tonight, for once, he did not mind.

CHAPTER 15: ROBERT'S NAME

The name in Marsh's working file pointed south.

Emma had spent three days with it, turning it over in the careful methodical way she turned over everything that required methodical care, building from the single line on page forty-one of the estate file toward whatever the name connected to. She had gone back to Dorothy Webb's archive and worked through the county records and the business filings and the professional licensing directories that existed in physical form at the historical society for exactly this kind of backward search, the kind of search that the grid going down had reduced to paper and physical records and the patient willingness to sit with incomplete information until it yielded what it had.

The name had a professional history. A Cincinnati accountant. Forty years of practice. Retired. Living, according to a professional directory from four years ago that Dorothy had found in the reference section, in a retirement community in Boone County, Kentucky.

Northern Kentucky. Forty-five minutes from Moores Hill under normal conditions.

Emma wrote the address in her custodian notebook and looked at it for a moment.

Then she went to find James.

***

She found him in the Carnegie Hall basement with the community resource map and the particular quality of controlled focus he had been carrying since the Thursday night operation, which had been three days ago and which he had documented with precise professional thoroughness and then set aside and moved forward from without visible ceremony. The girl was home. The community did not yet know the full story of how. James had decided the timing of that conversation mattered.

Emma understood the timing. She trusted his read on it.

"I need to go to Kentucky," she said. "Boone County. There's an accountant named Gerald Forsythe who handled the financial side of the Caldwell estate in parallel with Franklin Marsh's legal work. The name in Marsh's working file connects to Forsythe's professional history in a way I need to follow in person."

James looked at her with the assessing quality he brought to requests that had implications beyond the request itself.

"Boone County," he said. He said it the way he said things he was calculating as he said them. "That's twelve miles past the Kentucky line on roads that go through the Aurora corridor and then south." He looked at the map on the wall. "Since St. Leon the traffic on those roads has changed. We've had three reports from the checkpoint in the past four days of groups moving south and east, away from the highway corridor, looking for secondary routes. The Aurora road is a secondary route."

"I know," Emma said. "I'm not suggesting I drive it alone."

James looked at her.

"Talk to Danny," he said.

***

Danny McClanahan had been working on the truck for two weeks.

It had started as a practical response to what he was encountering on the mail run circuit. The county roads between Moores Hill and Lawrenceburg had been deteriorating in terms of the people on them, the organized desperation that James had described as structure developing in the weeks after the initial chaos, and Danny had come home from the second mail run in week three with a cracked windshield and a very clear understanding that an ordinary vehicle on those roads was becoming a liability.

He had talked to Gary Whitfield, who had talked to Tom Hargrove, and the three of them had spent a Saturday afternoon in Danny's barn with welding equipment and a supply of quarter-inch steel plate that Tom had located in his back inventory and donated without discussion.

The result was not elegant.

It was a 2009 Ford F-250 that had been transformed, through the application of serious intent and available materials, into something that a person might hesitate before approaching. Steel plate bolted to the interior of the cab doors. A welded steel grid over the rear window. The windshield backed with a steel frame that could accept a sheet of plate in an emergency, currently left open for visibility but ready. The bed fitted with plywood sides reinforced with steel angle iron that provided cover for anyone riding in the back.

Danny had driven it on the last three mail runs and had found that the people who had made the previous runs uncomfortable for him had a significantly different reaction to the truck than they had to an ordinary vehicle.

When Emma came to his house and told him what she needed, he walked her to the barn and showed her the truck and watched her look at it.

"How many people can ride in the back?" Emma said.

"Four comfortably," Danny said. "Six if they know each other."

Emma looked at him. "How many people has James given you for the mail runs?"

"Two," Danny said. "Gary's idea. Armed. Since St. Leon he's been putting two armed veterans on every run that goes outside the perimeter."

"I'll need the same for Kentucky," Emma said.

"More," Danny said. "Kentucky is further than Lawrenceburg and the roads between here and there go through ground we don't know as well." He looked at the truck. "I'll talk to Gary. We'll put four in the back."

Emma looked at the welded steel plate on the cab doors and thought about her drive to Cincinnati three weeks ago, the caravans on the county roads, the particular organized movement of people who had made decisions and were acting on them. That had been week four. This was week six. The trajectory between those two points was not moving in a comfortable direction.

"When can we go?" she said.

"Tomorrow morning," Danny said. "Early. Before the roads get active."

***

They left at five-thirty in the morning.

Danny driving, Emma in the passenger seat, four veterans in the reinforced bed behind them. Gary had selected them the previous evening with the same criteria he brought to everything that required trust under pressure, people he knew personally, people who understood the objective and who had the particular quality of steadiness that the objective required. They rode in the back without conversation, equipped with the hunting rifles and the specific situational awareness of people who had been on enough watch rotations to understand what watching required.

The pre-dawn roads were quiet in the way that early morning had always been quiet, the particular suspended quality of the hours before the world fully committed to the day. Emma watched the farms going past in the gray light and thought about what Danny had said about the roads getting active and what active meant on these particular roads in week six of the outage.

They passed the first group at the Aurora turnoff.

Eight people on foot, moving south on the shoulder of the county road with the specific loaded purposefulness of people who had been walking for more than a day and intended to keep walking. They turned to look at the truck as it passed. Emma watched them in the side mirror, the way their eyes followed the vehicle and then returned to the road ahead without lingering. They were not interested in the truck. They were interested in wherever they were going.

She thought about what they had left and what they were moving toward and whether whatever they were moving toward was going to be there when they arrived.

The second group was larger and moving in a different way.

They were stopped on the road two miles south of Aurora, a group of perhaps fifteen people, blocking the road not with intent but with the particular formlessness of people who had stopped moving and had not yet decided what to do next. They were standing or sitting on the roadside with the specific collapsed quality of exhaustion and uncertainty.

Danny slowed.

The people on the road looked at the truck the way the first group had looked at it, with the assessing quality of people who had been assessing every vehicle they encountered for weeks. But this group's assessment was different. Longer. More calculating. Emma watched it happen and understood what she was watching.

Danny did not stop. He found the gap in the group and moved through it at a speed that was slow enough to avoid hitting anyone and fast enough to not invite engagement, the particular calibrated pace that communicated movement and purpose without communicating aggression.

Nobody reached for the truck. Nobody moved to block it.

Emma heard one of the four in the back shift position as they moved through the group, the specific sound of someone adjusting their readiness without deploying it.

They cleared the group and Danny accelerated and Emma did not say anything and Danny did not say anything and the road ahead opened up into the gray morning light going south toward Kentucky.

"That's going to be worse on the way back," Gary said from the bed, his voice carrying through the rear window.

"Yes," Danny said.

"We'll take the ridge road back," Gary said. "Longer but less traffic."

Danny nodded.

Emma looked at the road ahead and thought about the folder she was going to come back with and what it was going to tell her and what she was going to do with what it told her.

***

The retirement community in Boone County had generator power.

She could see it from the access road, the specific quality of a facility that was functioning normally while everything around it was not, lights in the windows in the morning, the parking lot maintained, a staff member moving between buildings with the purposeful step of someone whose workday had continued without interruption. It had the particular quality, in the context of everything Emma had been living inside for six weeks, of something from a different time that had not yet understood that the time had changed.

Danny parked the truck in the visitor lot and stayed with it. Gary and one other veteran came inside with Emma. Not to intimidate. To be present, which in the current circumstances was a different kind of statement than it would have been six weeks ago.

The woman at the front desk looked at the three of them with the expression of someone who had been managing unusual situations since the outage began and had developed a specific threshold for what constituted unusual enough to require a different response.

Emma introduced herself and asked for Gerald Forsythe and gave the Caldwell estate as the reason.

The woman made the call. A pause. She put the phone down and gave Emma the room number and directions.

Gary and his colleague stayed in the lobby. Emma went alone.

***

Gerald Forsythe was eighty-one years old and carried his age in the particular way of people who had been physically active their entire lives and were still paying the dividend of that activity in their eighties, upright and deliberate in his movements, his hands steady, his eyes clear behind glasses that were slightly too large for his face in the style of a decade ago that he had apparently not seen a reason to update.

He answered the door with the expression of someone who had agreed to this visit without being entirely sure why and who was reserving judgment until he understood what he was dealing with.

Emma introduced herself.

His expression shifted when she gave her name. A small shift, the kind produced by a name connecting to a memory that had not been accessed recently, the specific quality of recognition arriving from somewhere that had been closed off for a long time.

"Caldwell," he said.

"Yes," Emma said. "Robert Caldwell was my father."

He looked at her for a moment with the careful assessment of someone recalibrating what he had been expecting against what was standing in front of him. Then he opened the door wider and stepped back.

"Come in," he said.

***

His room had the particular organized quality of someone who had spent a professional lifetime managing other people's financial affairs and had applied the same discipline to his own domestic space. Everything in its place. A small desk by the window with a neat stack of papers that appeared to be personal correspondence, written by hand in the careful script of someone for whom handwriting had always been a professional tool and who had not stopped using it with care simply because the professional context was gone.

He had a generator-powered coffee maker and he made coffee without asking whether she wanted it, setting two cups on the desk between them with the host's instinct of someone who understood that conversations of certain kinds went better with something to hold.

Emma sat across from him and waited.

He did not begin immediately. He sat with his coffee and looked at her with the assessing quality that forty years of financial practice produced, reading what he could of the situation from what was visible before committing to what he was going to say about it.

"You look like him," he said finally. "Around the eyes."

Emma was quiet for a moment. She let that land completely before she responded.

"Tell me what you remember about the estate," she said.

Forsythe set his coffee down. He looked at the window. At the view of the retirement community's maintained grounds, the grass cut and the beds tended by staff who were still showing up because the facility had its own infrastructure, a small island of function in a county that was managing the same sustained crisis as everywhere else.

"I handled the financial side of Robert Caldwell's estate in 2002," he said. "The legal work was with Franklin Marsh, whom I had worked with on several previous matters. The financial work came to me through Marsh as a referral. It was presented as a straightforward estate accounting job. Inventory the assets, document the values, prepare the distribution documentation."

"But it wasn't straightforward," Emma said.

"No," Forsythe said. He said it simply, without the defensiveness of someone protecting a professional reputation. He was eighty-one years old and his professional reputation was no longer the most important thing in the room. "It was the most unusual financial arrangement I handled in forty years of practice. I knew it at the time. I chose to proceed anyway."

Emma waited.

"The assets were real," he said. "That needs to be understood. The property, the accounts, the investments. All real, all properly documented, all legally belonging to the estate of Robert Caldwell as of the date of his reported death." He paused. "What was unusual was the destination of certain assets."

"They didn't transfer to the estate beneficiaries," Emma said.

Forsythe looked at her. "You've been doing your own research."

"Yes," Emma said.

"Then you may already know some of what I'm about to tell you." He picked up his coffee and held it without drinking. "A portion of the estate assets, not the majority but a significant portion, were redirected at the time of distribution into a series of accounts that I was instructed to establish and then never touch again. The accounts were structured in a specific way. Layered. With a particular architecture that I recognized even then as something designed for long-term operation rather than short-term holding."

"Designed by whom?" Emma said.

"By whoever had thought about this very carefully before the estate was filed," Forsythe said. "The instructions came through Marsh. Marsh told me they came from a party with authority over the estate's administration. He did not tell me who that party was and I did not ask." He said it plainly, the honest accounting of someone who had had twenty-three years to sit with a professional decision he had not made correctly. "I was paid well for my discretion. I maintained it for twenty-three years."

"Until now," Emma said.

"I'm eighty-one years old," Forsythe said. "The grid has been down for six weeks. I have been watching this facility manage its resources carefully while outside this community people are doing things I would not have believed six weeks ago." He looked at his hands on the desk. "Discretion has a statute of limitations. And you are his daughter."

"What name were the accounts registered under?" Emma said.

Forsythe was quiet for a moment. The kind of quiet that precedes the delivery of something that has been held for a long time and that is going to change when it is released.

He stood and went to his desk and opened the bottom drawer and removed a folder, thin and well-organized in the manner of a man who kept important things accessible, and brought it back to the table between them.

"I kept a copy of the account structures," he said. "Against my instructions, I kept a copy. Because in forty years of practice I had learned that the records you were told to destroy were sometimes the ones that mattered most." He opened the folder and turned it toward her.

Emma looked at the documents.

The account architecture was exactly what she had expected from what Forsythe had described. Layered. Designed for long-term operation. The kind of financial structure that a person built when they intended to disappear from one identity and continue operating under another, when they needed resources to move through the world without those resources being traceable to the name they had left behind. Built with the specific care of someone who understood what they were building and why it needed to last.

At the top of the first page, in the registration line, a name.

Not Robert Caldwell.

A name she had never heard. A name with no connection to Moores Hill or Indiana or anything in her life. A name that had been chosen with the specific care of someone who understood that a new identity needed to be completely disconnected from the old one to be safe.

She read it.

She read it again.

She wrote it in her custodian notebook beneath the name from Marsh's working file and looked at the two names side by side.

Two names. One pointing at the financial architecture. One pointing at the person who had known the death was coming before it happened. Both connected to the same estate. Both pointing, from different directions, at the same man.

"The account structure," she said. "Over twenty-three years. Is it still active?"

Forsythe looked at her with the expression of someone who had been waiting for exactly this question.

"I don't know," he said. "I set it up. I walked away as instructed. What happened to it after that is beyond what I can tell you." He paused. "But the architecture was built to last. Whoever designed it understood that they were building something for the long term. If it has been maintained, and if the person running it understood what they were doing, then yes. It would still be active."

Emma looked at the documents on the table between them. At the layered account structure. At the name that was not her father's name but that was her father's life.

She thought about twenty-three years of patient monitoring. About a ghost pattern in the missing persons databases keyed to the coordinates of seven sacred sites, built and maintained with the same patient thoroughness as the financial architecture she was looking at. About a man in Peru who had built an entirely parallel existence around a mission that he had decided was more important than the family he had left behind, who had funded that existence through an account structure that a retired accountant in Boone County, Kentucky had been keeping a copy of for twenty-three years against instructions.

About what it cost to make a decision like that and live inside it for longer than Emma had been alive.

She closed the folder.

"Thank you," she said. She meant it completely and without qualification.

Forsythe nodded. He looked at the folder on the table. "Take it," he said. "I've been keeping it long enough. It belongs with you now."

Emma put the folder in her bag and stood and shook his hand and went back through the facility to the lobby where Gary was waiting and out through the main entrance to the parking lot where Danny had the truck running and the four veterans in the back were watching the access road with the focused patience of people who had been on watch rotation long enough to be patient without being inattentive.

She got in.

Danny looked at her.

She nodded once.

He put the truck in gear.

***

They took the ridge road back.

Gary had been right that the county road would be worse on the return trip and the ridge road added fifteen minutes but moved through terrain that was less traveled and less observed, the particular back roads of southern Dearborn County that Danny knew from seven weeks of daily circuits and that the people who were moving through the region on the primary roads did not know well enough to use.

Emma sat in the passenger seat with her bag in her lap and the folder inside it and looked at the ridge road moving through the morning light and thought about everything she had assembled.

Two names. One financial architecture built for decades of operation. One lawyer's notation from three weeks before a death that had never happened. The ghost pattern in the databases. The twenty-three years of monitoring. The letters to the custodian family that she had not yet told her father she had sent and that he had apparently been reading before the family responded.

That last piece.

He had been reading her letters before she knew he was reading them. Which meant he knew about Montana. About Carnegie Hall.

About the Ashcraft conversation and the box and the letter in English dated 1887. About the investigation she had been conducting into his estate records.

About her.

She thought about sitting in a room in Peru, reading letters from a daughter you believed did not know you existed, watching her piece together the architecture of the life you had built to protect her from what you knew and watching her find the edges of it anyway because she was exactly the kind of person you had left behind.

She thought about what that felt like from the inside.

She did not let herself feel it from his side for long. She was not ready for that. She filed it in the place she filed things she was not ready for and returned to what she had.

The conclusion was no longer a conclusion supported by evidence. It was a certainty. Her father was alive. He was in Peru. He had been watching the seven sites and her work for long enough to understand what she was doing before she had finished doing it. He had read her letters to the custodian family. He knew she was alive and working and had found the edges of what he had built.

And he had not reached out.

She thought about that too.

She filed it in the same place.

***

Danny pulled onto Oak Street at half past nine in the morning and stopped in front of Carnegie Hall and Emma got out and thanked each of the four veterans in the bed by name and thanked Danny and went inside.

She set up at her east window table. Rufus settled under it immediately, his chin on her foot, his weight the specific familiar weight of an animal who had decided that being present was the most useful thing he could offer and who was offering it completely.

She spread what she had across the table.

The Marsh file. The Forsythe folder. The custodian notebook open to the page with the two names. The three questions she had written beneath them a week ago.

Who are you.

How did you know.

Where did the money come from.

She had the answers to all three now.

She looked at them for a long time. At the complete picture assembled from three months of investigation conducted through physical records and in-person conversations and the patient application of a data security analyst's understanding of how systems left traces even when they were designed not to.

Her mother had spent thirty-plus years protecting Carnegie Hall without knowing the full scope of why. Her father had spent twenty-three years building a monitoring network across seven sacred sites without knowing his daughter had found the knowledge from the other end and was rebuilding what he had been watching from the inside.

Two people doing the same work from opposite sides of the world without knowing about each other until recently.

She thought about what that said about the work itself. About the thing that had drawn both of them toward it through completely different paths. About the specific pull of a mission that was larger than any single person's life and that had a way of finding the people it needed regardless of whether those people had been looking for it.

She closed the notebook.

She opened it again to a fresh page.

She picked up her pen and began to write the letter she had been composing in the back of her mind since she sat across from Gerald

Forsythe and read a name that was not her father's name but that was her father's life.

She was not ready to meet him.

But she was ready to write.

And she wrote with the full weight of everything she knew, which was more than she had known yesterday and less than she would know tomorrow, and she wrote honestly, because she was Emma Caldwell and honesty was the only language she had ever trusted completely.

She wrote until the morning light through the east windows had moved to afternoon light and Rufus had shifted twice beneath the table and Margaret Hendricks had come by once to set a cup of coffee beside her without saying anything because Margaret Hendricks understood the difference between someone who needed to be interrupted and someone who needed to be left alone to finish something.

When she finished she read it back.

Then she folded it carefully and addressed the envelope to the post office box and put it in her bag to take to Gerald Sims in the morning.

She sat at the table in the afternoon light with Carnegie Hall quiet around her and thought about a man in Peru who was going to read this letter in a few weeks and who was going to have to decide, when he read it, what came next.

She did not envy him that decision.

But she did not take it back either.

***

Twenty days.

She had stopped doing the exercises four days ago. Not because she had given up. Because the food had gotten slightly less and the energy required for the exercises had started costing more than she could reliably replace and she had made a calculation about conservation that her gym teacher would have understood even if she could not have explained it in those terms.

She slept more now. Not because she was more tired, though she was more tired, but because sleep was the most efficient way to make time pass without using resources she needed for waking. She had read something once about hibernation, about how animals slowed their metabolism in winter to survive on less, and she thought about that sometimes when she was trying to sleep in the middle of the day.

She was not hibernating. She was conserving.

There was a difference and the difference mattered to her even if it would not have mattered to anyone else.

The marks on the wall had started to look like a lot. Twenty of them in a careful row. She had not imagined, on the first night when she had decided that paying attention was the job, that there would be twenty marks. She had not let herself imagine a number. Imagining a number and then passing it was the kind of thing that broke the mechanism she had built to stay functional and she needed the mechanism more than she needed the comfort of imagining it would end soon.

She did not know if anyone was coming.

She knew that her parents knew she was gone. She knew that because knowing anything else was not compatible with conserving and she had chosen conservation over despair on the first night and had not changed that choice.

She knew her parents knew she was gone.

What she did not know was whether knowing was enough.

She pulled the blanket around her shoulders and added the twentieth mark to the row and put the stone back in its corner and lay down on the sleeping pad and listened to the sounds of the facility and thought about the third step on the staircase to the second floor and the way everyone stepped over it automatically without looking and how she was going to step over it exactly that way when she got back.

When.

She held that word carefully in the dark.

When.

She closed her eyes.

Outside the grain facility, in the dark of a July night in Indiana, the community that had been managing its crisis for ten weeks went about its careful quiet business.

Twelve miles away James McClanahan drove the farm circuit and did not yet know exactly where she was.

But he was getting closer.

CHAPTER 16: COMING HOME

Danny drove without headlights for the first mile past the grain facility.

Not because James had told him to. Because Danny understood, without being told, that the county road between the facility and Moores Hill was a road that people used at night for reasons that were not good reasons, and that a vehicle moving without lights through that particular stretch was less visible and therefore less interesting than a vehicle announcing itself, and that less interesting was better than more interesting when the bed of the truck contained four veterans standing down from an operation and the back seat contained a girl who had been through three weeks of captivity and who was sitting with Carol Beatty's hands on her and her face turned toward the window watching the dark fields go past.

Carol had done her assessment in the first two minutes after the east wall exit. Dehydration, manageable. Malnourishment, significant but not critical. The specific psychological state of someone who had been held long enough that the holding had become normalized and who was now in the disorientation that followed its removal. Carol had communicated all of it to James with a single nod, the practiced economy of a combat medic who understood that the field report needed to be delivered in the time available for it, which was approximately one second.

She was okay. She was going to be okay.

James carried that with him through the dark mile and the turn onto the county road and the moment Danny turned the headlights on and the familiar ground ahead came into view.

He turned and looked at her through the rear window.

She was watching the road. At the headlights making the county road visible in the dark. At the particular quality of the Indiana night going about its business around a truck full of people bringing her home. Her face carried the specific expression of someone who was not yet fully present in the moment she was in, who was still partly in the grain facility and the three weeks before it, processing the removal of a reality that had been her entire world for long enough to feel like the only world.

Carol said something to her quietly. She turned from the window and looked at Carol and said something back.

James faced forward.

They drove the rest of the way to Moores Hill in silence.

***

He did not take her straight home.

This was a decision he had made during the four days of preparation, one of the decisions that did not appear in any operational plan but that he had understood would need to be made. A girl returned from captivity in the middle of the night needed to be assessed properly before she was delivered to her parents, not because the assessment mattered more than the reunion but because the reunion would go better if the assessment came first. Her parents had been living with four-day exchanges at a grain elevator for three weeks. What they needed, when they saw their daughter, was to see that she was whole.

He took her to Carol's house first.

Carol had set up a space in her front room the way a field medic set up a treatment space, everything accessible, everything in order, the specific organized calm of a professional who had decided how she was going to approach this before it arrived. She worked through the assessment with the thoroughness she brought to everything and the particular gentleness she brought to this specific kind of situation, talking to the girl throughout in the low steady voice that was not quite clinical and not quite personal but somewhere between the two that was exactly right.

An hour. James sat in Carol's kitchen and drank coffee that Carol had made before they left and thought about nothing specific, which was its own kind of discipline, the discipline of not thinking ahead to the things that needed to happen next until the thing that was happening now was finished.

Carol came to the kitchen door.

"She's ready," Carol said. "She needs real food and real sleep and a few weeks of being home. But she's ready."

James drove her home in the truck with Carol beside her and Danny behind the wheel and the first gray suggestion of dawn beginning at the eastern edge of the sky.

***

The collaborator answered the door before he knocked.

They had been awake. Of course they had been awake. James had not told them tonight was the night because he had not known tonight was the night until the dead drop observation confirmed what he needed confirmed, and by the time he had assembled the team and executed and brought the girl to Carol's house and waited out the assessment, it was three-thirty in the morning and the possibility that they had slept through any of it was essentially zero.

They stood in the doorway and looked at their daughter and made a sound that James had no word for, a sound that was below language and above silence, the specific human sound of a relief so complete it could not find its shape in any available form of expression.

He stepped back from the door.

He had been in rooms where significant things happened. He had learned over the years the ability to be present in those rooms without being moved in ways that compromised his function. He stood on the porch of this farmhouse in the pre-dawn dark and listened to what was happening inside and felt the particular exhausted satisfaction of someone who had done the right thing in exactly the right way and who understood, without needing to examine it, that this was what the work was for.

Carol came out after a few minutes and stood beside him on the porch.

"She's going to be okay," Carol said again. Not because she needed to say it again. Because it was worth saying twice.

"Yes," James said.

He waited until he could hear from inside the house that the initial intensity of the reunion had moved toward something quieter and more sustainable. Then he knocked softly on the open door and the collaborator came to it and James told them what had happened at the facility in the plain factual language he used for things that needed to be documented and understood clearly. Four men secured. The facility location known to Reeves. The two who had escaped the Miller farm incident were still at large but the core of the local operation was neutralized.

The collaborator listened with the expression of someone receiving information that their nervous system had not yet fully caught up to. Three weeks of impossible weight setting down all at once produced its own kind of disorientation.

"What happens now?" they said. "To us. To the community."

James looked at them for a moment.

"That conversation needs to happen with the community," he said. "Not tonight. In a few days, when she's had time to be home and you've had time to think about how to tell it." He paused. "The community is going to need to hear the full story. Not a version of it. The full story. I think when they do, most of them will understand. Some of them won't. But everyone will know."

The collaborator nodded slowly. "Will you be there?"

"Yes," James said. "I'll be there."

He left them to the morning and drove back to Carnegie Hall as the first genuine light of dawn began to separate the tree lines from the sky.

He went to the basement. He sat at the desk. He opened his notebook and began to write up everything that had happened in the precise methodical language of a former deputy who understood that documentation was how the work survived.

He was still writing when the shot rang out.

***

It was a .22. He knew it by the sound, the specific sharp crack of a small caliber rifle that was different from the heavier report of the hunting rifles the watch positions carried. He was out of the basement and through the Carnegie Hall front door in fifteen seconds, moving toward the sound, which had come from the direction of Oak Street.

What he found when he came around the corner stopped him.

Owen Mitchell was on the ground in the middle of Oak Street.

Not dead. Sitting up, actually, with the specific expression of a man who had been surprised by something and was still in the process of deciding how he felt about it. He was thinner than James remembered and his clothes had the specific quality of garments that had been through significant use since they were last washed and he had a graze on his left forearm that was bleeding in the unhurried way of a wound that was not serious but was definitely present.

Beside him, attached to a lead rope that Owen was still somehow holding, was a mule.

The mule was standing at the far end of the lead rope with its ears back and the specific expression of an animal that had recently been startled and had registered its objection to that experience and was now considering its options.

On her porch, in pajamas, holding a .22 rifle with the barrel pointed at the sky and her mouth open in an expression that James had never seen on Emma Caldwell's face before and that he could only describe as the precise intersection of horror and disbelief, was Emma.

James looked at Owen.

Owen looked at James.

"She shot me," Owen said. He said it with the particular tone of a man who was reporting a fact that he had not yet fully processed. "Emma Caldwell shot me off a mule."

"I thought you were the farmer," Emma said from the porch. Her voice had the specific quality of someone who was still not entirely sure they were awake.

"I'm not the farmer," Owen said.

"I know that now," Emma said.

James looked at the mule. The mule looked back at James with the profound indifference of an animal that had been through enough in the past several weeks to find this particular situation only moderately remarkable.

"Owen," James said. "When did you get back?"

"Approximately forty-five seconds ago," Owen said. "I was going to knock on your door." He looked at his arm. "I didn't get that far."

From inside the house came the sound of claws on hardwood and then the screen door pushed open in the specific way it pushed open when something with four legs and no hands had learned the trick of it.

Rufus came down the porch steps at a measured pace. Not the urgent scramble of a dog responding to a crisis. The deliberate unhurried movement of an animal that had heard what was happening and had decided it had something to say about it.

He ignored James. He ignored Emma. He ignored the mule, which was remarkable given that the mule was the largest thing on Oak Street.

He walked directly to Owen and stopped in front of him and looked at him.

Owen looked back at Rufus.

They regarded each other for a moment with the specific quality of two parties who had unfinished business and both knew it.

"Rufus," Owen said. The tone of a man who understood what was coming and was hoping against reasonable hope.

Rufus looked at Owen's boot.

"Don't," Owen said.

Rufus lifted his leg.

Owen looked at the sky with the expression of a man who had ridden a mule from Colorado to Indiana, been shot off it by his own business partner, and had just run out of remaining dignity entirely.

Then Rufus did something he had not done in six weeks.

He stepped forward and put his chin on Owen's knee and stayed there. His tail moved in the slow steady arc that meant something specific and everyone who knew Rufus understood what it meant.

Owen put his hand on the dog's head.

Neither of them moved for a moment.

"He missed you," Emma said from the porch. Her voice had changed.

"Yeah," Owen said. His voice had changed too. "I missed him."

James looked at the two of them and then looked at Emma on the porch in her pajamas with the .22 still in her hand and then looked at the mule standing at the end of the lead rope with its ears back.

"Let's get you inside," James said.

***

The sun came up on a scene that would be described, retold, and refined in its retelling for as long as anyone who had been present for it remained in Moores Hill.

Carol Beatty came out of her house two doors down when she heard the shot, still in her own clothes from the night's operation, her medical kit in her hand because Carol Beatty's response to any loud noise in the current circumstances was to bring the medical kit. She looked at Owen on the ground and the mule at the end of the lead rope and Emma on the porch and James standing in the street and said: "Is anyone actually hurt?"

"Grazed," Owen said.

Carol crouched beside him and looked at the arm with the efficiency of someone who had been assessing wounds all night and had not yet stopped. "It's nothing," she said. "You'll live."

"I was aware of that," Owen said.

Danny McClanahan, who had been driving back from dropping the veterans at their respective houses, turned onto Oak Street and stopped his truck and got out and looked at the scene in front of him with the expression of a man who had been awake for twenty-three hours and was no longer confident that what he was seeing was real.

"Is that a mule?" Danny said.

"Yes," James said.

"Why does Owen have a mule?"

"That," Owen said from the ground, "is an extremely long story."

Margaret Hendricks appeared at the end of the block, drawn by the shot the way Margaret was drawn by anything that suggested the community needed information managed, and stopped when she saw Owen and looked at Emma on the porch and looked at the mule and said nothing for a moment, which was unusual for Margaret.

Then she started laughing.

Not the polite contained laugh of a woman managing a public situation. The full genuine laugh of someone who had been holding the weight of six weeks of community crisis and had just been handed something so perfectly absurd that the weight had no choice but to let go of itself. She laughed with her hand over her mouth and then with both hands and then without either hand because both hands were needed to keep her upright.

It spread the way laughter spread in small communities, which was immediately and completely. Danny started. Then Carol, who was still crouched beside Owen wrapping his arm with the bandaging from her kit and who began laughing in the specific way of someone trying very hard not to laugh while performing a medical procedure. Reeves appeared from the direction of Carnegie Hall, took in the scene in one sweep, and made a sound that was attempting to be professional and was not succeeding.

Owen looked around at all of them.

"I would like to point out," he said, "that I rode a mule from western Colorado to southeastern Indiana to get home. I crossed three mountain ranges. I survived two encounters with people who wanted to take the mule and everything I had left. I traded my Rolex for passage through a particularly difficult stretch of Kansas." He paused. "And I get home and Emma Caldwell shoots me."

Emma had come off the porch. She was standing in the street now, still in her pajamas, still holding the .22, with the expression of someone who was oscillating rapidly between mortification and the specific helpless laughter that arrived when mortification reached a level that the body could no longer contain.

"I thought you were the ghost," she said. Her voice was slightly unsteady.

"I am not a ghost," Owen said.

"It was dark," Emma said.

"It is slightly less dark now," Owen said. "And I am still not a ghost."

Emma looked at him. At the mule. At the graze on his arm that Carol was finishing wrapping with the brisk efficiency of someone who had treated worse things in the past six hours and was not going to pretend otherwise.

"Owen," she said.

"Emma," he said.

"I'm sorry I shot you," she said.

Owen looked at her for a long moment. At the pajamas and the .22 and the expression on her face that was doing three things at once and not quite managing any of them.

"It's fine," he said. He said it the way people said things that were not entirely fine but that they had decided to treat as fine because the alternative was a conversation that neither of them was ready to have at five in the morning in the middle of Oak Street. "Help me up."

Emma put out her hand and Owen took it and she helped him to his feet and he stood and brushed the dust of Oak Street off his clothes and looked at Moores Hill coming awake in the early morning light around him.

He had been gone six weeks. The town looked the same and felt completely different, the specific difference of a place that has been through something significant and carries it in the way its people move and look at each other and occupy their shared spaces.

He looked at James.

"Tell me everything," Owen said.

"It's a long story," James said.

"I have time," Owen said. "I appear to have nothing but time." He looked at the mule, who was standing placidly at the end of its lead rope eating something it had found at the edge of the road. "Someone is going to need to explain to me what to do with this animal."

"I know a farm," Danny said.

The mule looked up from its roadside breakfast and regarded the assembled citizens of Moores Hill with the profound philosophical indifference of an animal that had traveled a very long distance and had arrived somewhere and was currently eating and considered that a satisfactory outcome regardless of what the humans around it thought about anything.

James looked at the scene around him.

At Owen standing in the street in clothes that had been through everything. At Emma in her pajamas with her hand still half-extended from pulling him up, her face settling from its three-way oscillation into something that was mostly relief with a residue of mortification that was going to take a few days to fully clear. At Margaret Hendricks still laughing at the end of the block. At Carol finishing the bandage with the brisk efficiency that was her baseline mode of operation. At Danny looking at the mule with the specific expression of someone who had been asked to find a solution to an unexpected problem and was already finding it.

At Moores Hill coming awake in the early morning light around all of them.

He thought about the girl asleep in her parents' house two streets over. About the six weeks this community had been through. About the things that were still ahead of it and the things it had already survived.

He thought about Owen riding a mule from western Colorado to southeastern Indiana because home was home and there was no other direction worth traveling.

He thought about Emma on her porch in her pajamas shooting the ghost of the farmer off his mule.

And James McClanahan, who had not laughed in six weeks, laughed.

It started small and it did not stay small and he did not try to make it stay small because some things were worth laughing at completely and this was one of them and the community around him had earned it and so had he.

Owen looked at him.

"I'm glad," Owen said, with the dry precision that was his particular gift, "that my suffering is bringing everyone such joy."

Which made it worse.

Which was exactly right.

CHAPTER 17: THE RIGHT QUESTION

Emma did not sleep after the shooting.

This was not a surprise. She lay in bed in the early morning with the .22 back in its place against the living room wall and Rufus beside her on the bed in the specific position he took when he had decided she needed company rather than space, pressed against her from shoulder to knee with the warm solid weight of an animal who understood that presence was its own kind of help, and she stared at the ceiling and thought about Owen Mitchell on the ground in Oak Street with blood on his arm and a mule at the end of a rope.

She had shot Owen Mitchell.

She had stood on her porch in her pajamas in the pre-dawn dark still half inside the Irish Bowl nightmare and she had seen a figure on a mule in the street below her and she had done the thing that six weeks of living inside a crisis had apparently done to her reflexes, which was to reach for the .22 before the conscious mind had finished forming the question of whether reaching for the .22 was the appropriate response.

It had not been the appropriate response.

She thought about Owen's face when he looked up from the ground and said she shot me with the specific tone of a man reporting a fact he had not yet processed. She thought about the way the whole street had laughed, the genuine uncontrollable laughter of a community releasing six weeks of accumulated weight through the most perfectly absurd thing that had happened to any of them since the grid went down.

She thought about James laughing.

She thought about the three of them. James. Owen. Her. Clue-Minati Investigative Services, LLC, operating out of Moores Hill, Indiana. James the former deputy with twelve years of law enforcement experience. Owen the former investigative reporter who had left the Columbus Dispatch to go independent. Emma the former data security analyst who had left Nashville to come home and had never quite left again. Three people who had decided that their particular combination of skills was useful and had been right about that in ways none of them had fully anticipated.

She had shot one of her business partners off a mule.

In spite of everything she felt the specific helpless laughter building again in her chest and she pressed her face into Rufus's fur and let it come because there was nobody to see it and because it was better out than in.

Rufus tolerated this with the dignity he brought to all of Emma's less composed moments.

She gave up on sleep at six and got dressed and went to the diner.

***

Sarah McClanahan had been open since five.

The diner ran on the propane setup that Sarah had installed two years ago for reasons she had not been able to fully articulate at the time and that had turned out to be one of the more consequential decisions anyone in Moores Hill had made before the grid went down. It had become, over six weeks, something more than a diner. It was the place people came in the mornings when the day ahead felt too large for the space of a single household, the warmth of it and the smell of the cooking and the particular quality of Sarah McClanahan's presence behind the counter, which was the presence of someone who had been feeding people through difficult times her whole professional life and who understood that the act of feeding someone was its own kind of statement about what a community owed its members.

Owen was at the counter.

Of course he was at the counter. Emma stood in the diner doorway for a moment and looked at him, at the back of his head and the clothes that had been through everything and the specific posture of someone who had been given a plate of real food after weeks of whatever he had been surviving on and who was experiencing that plate with a focus that did not have room for anything else.

Sarah looked up from the counter and saw Emma and her expression did a complicated thing that contained amusement and sympathy in approximately equal measure.

Owen heard the door and turned on his stool.

He looked at Emma.

Emma looked at Owen.

"Good morning," Emma said.

"Is it," Owen said. He said it without the inflection that would have made it a question. He turned back to his plate.

Emma sat down two stools away, the specific distance of someone who understood that two stools was close enough to be clearly intentional and far enough to give the other person room to decide what they wanted the distance to be.

Sarah set a cup of coffee in front of her without being asked. Emma wrapped both hands around it and looked at the counter.

"Owen," she said.

"Emma," he said, without turning.

"I'm sorry," she said. "I was having the nightmare and I saw you in the dark and I thought--"

"You thought I was the ghost of the farmer," Owen said.

"Yes," Emma said.

Owen was quiet for a moment. He took a bite of whatever Sarah had made him, which appeared to be eggs and the particular preserved pork that had been a community staple for the past three weeks, and chewed with the meditative focus of someone extracting maximum value from every bite.

"In my defense," Emma said, "you were on a mule."

Owen turned on his stool and looked at her. His face did a complicated thing. The effort of maintaining the aggrieved expression he had apparently decided was the appropriate response to being shot fought visibly with something else, the something else winning incrementally, until what remained was the particular expression of a man who had ridden a mule from Colorado and been shot off it by Emma Caldwell and who had, somewhere in the past hour, accepted that this was simply a thing that had happened in his life.

"I was on a mule," he confirmed.

"A very convincing mule," Emma said.

"All mules are convincing," Owen said. "That's the nature of mules."

Sarah made a sound behind the counter that was attempting to be something other than laughter and was not entirely succeeding.

Owen looked at Emma for a moment longer. Then he turned back to his plate. "Sit closer," he said. "You're going to make me talk loudly and I don't have the energy for loudly."

Emma moved one stool. The specific one stool that was not two stools and was not adjacent, the distance of people who were comfortable with each other in the complicated way that their history produced.

"Also," Owen said, without looking up from his plate, "you shot your own business partner."

"I'm aware," Emma said.

"I want that noted."

"It's noted."

Sarah refilled Owen's coffee and did not attempt to hide the smile this time.

***

He told her about the road.

Not immediately. He finished his plate first with the focused attention of someone who had learned over six weeks not to take a full plate for granted, and Sarah took the plate away and brought him another without being asked, smaller this time, because Sarah McClanahan understood the specific dietary situation of someone who had been seriously undernourished and knew that the second plate needed to be smaller than the first regardless of what the person in front of her thought they could manage.

Owen looked at the second plate and then at Sarah.

"Eat it slowly," Sarah said, in the tone she used for things that were not suggestions.

Owen ate it slowly.

Then he wrapped both hands around his coffee cup and looked at the counter for a moment and began.

He had been in Telluride when the grid went down. A contact, he said, someone he had been developing for a piece he was working on for the agency. He had rented a car and driven east immediately, understanding within the first hours that what was happening was not a localized event and that east was the only direction that made sense.

He had made it to Kansas before the car became a liability.

It was not a single incident. It was the accumulation of several incidents over three days, the specific calculation that changed when you were driving through a region that had been without power for two weeks and that was reorganizing itself around the new reality of what resources were available and who had them. A vehicle that ran and had fuel was a resource. The people who understood that best were not always the people he wanted to have that conversation with.

He traded the car in western Kansas for a horse and two weeks of food and the name of a man in Missouri who was rumored to have additional horses available.

"The horse died in Missouri," he said.

He said it simply. Emma looked at her coffee and did not say anything.

It had been a good horse, Owen said, after a moment. Not young. But steady and willing and it had gotten him through Kansas and most of Missouri without complaint and had died in a field outside of a town he could not remember the name of in the specific way that animals died when they had been pushed past what they had left to give. He had sat with it for a while. Then he had gotten up and walked east.

He had traded the Rolex in a town in eastern Missouri.

There was a group managing a stretch of the highway there, he said. Not hostile exactly. Organized. They had a toll system and the toll system had a specific list of what they accepted and the Rolex was on the list and the highway passage was what he needed and the calculation had taken approximately four seconds.

"And the ring?" Emma said quietly.

Owen was quiet for a moment.

He had found the mule at a farm outside of a small town in Missouri, he said. An older farmer who had a mule he was willing to part with and who had looked at Owen with the particular assessment of a man who understood that the person in front of him had something worth trading and was deciding what he wanted for the mule.

The farmer had looked at the ring.

Owen had looked at the farmer. At the mule. At his hand.

He had thought about Sarah Bennett, who had been murdered by a man who believed his own desires entitled him to other people's lives and who had been wrong about that in ways he had not lived to fully understand. He had thought about what Sarah would have said if she could have seen him standing in a Missouri field with a ring on his finger and a mule in front of him and a thousand miles still between him and home.

He knew what she would have said.

He put the lead rope in his hand and walked east.

He said none of this directly. He said it in the specific way that Owen Mitchell said things that mattered deeply to him, which was in the spaces between the words, in what he did not say and in the quality of silence he left around the things he did say. Emma had known him long enough to read those spaces. She read them now and did not try to fill them with anything because there was nothing available to her that was adequate and she was self-aware enough to know it.

They sat with it for a moment.

Sarah moved to the far end of the counter with the particular tact of someone who understood exactly what kind of conversation was happening and what it required of her.

"You rode a mule from Missouri to Indiana," Emma said finally.

"Missouri to Indiana," Owen confirmed. "Through Illinois. Which I do not recommend."

"How long?"

"Three weeks," Owen said. "Give or take. The mule is more opinionated than the horse was but considerably more durable." He paused. "Her name is Margaret."

Emma looked at him.

"I named her after Margaret Hendricks," Owen said. "They have a similar quality of determination."

Emma thought about Margaret Hendricks at the information table in Carnegie Hall, dispensing knowledge and coffee and the particular brand of calm authority that had been holding the community's informational center together for six weeks, and about a mule plodding steadily east through Illinois with Owen Mitchell on her back.

"I think Margaret would be flattered," Emma said.

"Margaret the mule seems to feel she has earned the name," Owen said.

Sarah came back with the coffee pot and filled both cups and this time she did stay, leaning on the counter with her arms crossed, because the part of the conversation that required privacy had apparently passed and the part that was simply Owen being home had arrived and Sarah McClanahan was not going to miss Owen being home.

***

They sat with it for a moment.

Sarah moved to the far end of the counter with the particular tact of someone who understood exactly what kind of conversation was happening and what it required of her.

Owen picked up his coffee. Emma picked up hers. Outside the diner windows Moores Hill was going about its Saturday morning with the adapted efficiency of a community that had been doing this for six weeks and had found its rhythm. People on foot. Danny McClanahan's truck turning onto Main Street from the direction of the post office. The particular quality of a small town that had been through something significant and was still standing.

"So," Owen said.

"So," Emma said.

"Clue-Minati is still a going concern?"

"We have an office," Emma said. "Tom Hargrove is using it to store canned goods but it's still ours."

Owen considered this. "That seems about right for where we are." He looked at his coffee. "What are you working on?"

Emma looked at him. At the custodian notebook sitting on the counter between them where she had set it without consciously deciding to set it there. Owen looked at it too. Then back at her.

"That's a long answer," Emma said.

"I rode a mule from Colorado," Owen said. "I have time."

Emma opened the notebook.

She had gotten three pages in when the diner door opened and Rufus came through it.

Not with Emma. On his own, which was a thing Rufus occasionally did when he had decided that Emma had been somewhere long enough and he had opinions about it. He had learned the diner door with determined efficiency from the start. Sarah had never once tried to stop him because Sarah McClanahan's position on dogs in her diner was that dogs had better manners than most of her customers and she stood by that assessment.

Rufus came to Emma's stool first. Assessed her. Decided she was fine. Then turned and found Owen.

He looked at Owen for a long moment with the full quality of his attention, which was considerable.

Owen looked back at him.

"Hello Rufus," Owen said.

Rufus tilted his head approximately twelve degrees to the right. His ears were fully forward. His tail was doing the thing it had been doing on Oak Street two hours ago, the steady unhurried arc of an animal who had made a decision about how he felt about a situation.

Then he walked to Owen's stool and put his chin on Owen's knee and stayed there.

Owen looked down at him. Something moved across his face that he did not try to manage.

He put his hand on the dog's head.

They stayed like that for a moment. Sarah kept her back to the counter. Her shoulders were still.

Then Rufus lifted his head, returned to Emma's side, and sat down with the composed patience of an animal who had handled a piece of business and was now ready to move on.

"Tell me about the notebook," Owen said.

Emma turned the page.

Outside Sarah McClanahan's diner Moores Hill went about its morning. The community that had been through six weeks of sustained crisis moving through its adapted routines with the quiet efficiency of people who had found their rhythm inside a difficult reality.

And at the counter of the diner, over coffee that Sarah kept refilling without being asked, with Margaret the mule tied to the post outside and Rufus settled between their stools with his chin on his paws, Emma Caldwell told Owen Mitchell the full arc of what she had been working on.

For the first time since the grid went down she was not working alone.

It felt exactly right.

CHAPTER 18: THE COMMUNITY RECKONING

James had been carrying it for sixteen days.

Not because he was uncertain about telling the community. He had never been uncertain about that. A community managing a sustained crisis on the basis of shared information and mutual trust had the right to know when that information had been compromised and why.

What he had spent time on was the question of when.

The girl needed to be home first. Not just physically home, but home in the sense that mattered more, the sense of a person who had been through something significant and had been given enough time and quiet and enough of the ordinary rhythms of her own household to begin the process of becoming themselves again. He had checked in with Carol Beatty every three days. Carol's assessment had moved from she needs time to she's finding her footing to this week she laughed at something her father said and meant it.

That was the signal he had been waiting for.

He spoke to the collaborator first. The same kitchen table, the same afternoon light, the same two cups of coffee that neither of them drank. He told them what was going to happen and when and what he was going to say and gave them the choice of how they wanted to be present for it. In the room or not in the room.

They said they would be there.

He scheduled the meeting for Thursday at noon.

***

Word moved through Moores Hill the way word always moved through Moores Hill, which was immediately and completely. By Wednesday evening everyone in town knew that James

McClanahan had called a full community meeting for Thursday noon and that it was not the daily briefing and that it was about something specific he had not yet disclosed.

Nobody was speculating about what had actually happened. The collaborator had held it completely for sixteen days. He filed that and carried it into Thursday.

***

Carnegie Hall filled faster than the Day 1 meeting.

By eleven-thirty the hall held close to two hundred people. Margaret Hendricks had not set up her information table at James's request. This was a different kind of meeting and it needed to feel different from the moment people walked through the door.

James stood at the front without notes.

He found the collaborator in the crowd before he began. Seated in the middle of the hall, not hidden, not in the back row, exactly where James had told them to sit. Their face carried the expression of someone who had made a decision about how to do a difficult thing and was doing it.

He looked away from them and looked at the room.

"Six weeks ago this community made a decision to manage a crisis together," he said. "You shared information. You shared resources. You trusted each other with things that mattered. That trust is the reason Moores Hill has functioned the way it has while communities around us have not."

He paused.

"I need to tell you about something that happened inside that trust. I'm going to tell you the full story."

The room was very quiet.

He told them.

The checkpoint approach in week two. The daughter who had not come home from Lawrenceburg. The note under the back door. The dead drop at the grain elevator. The photographs. The sixteen exchanges over three weeks. The specific information that had been passed and what it had cost the community in terms of resources targeted and security compromised.

And then who had passed it and why.

He said the name.

The room received it the way rooms received significant information, not all at once but in a wave. James watched it move through the hall and did not say anything until it finished.

Then he waited.

***

Ruth Saylor spoke first

She was seventy-three years old and had lived in Moores Hill her entire life and she did not stand up slowly the way some people her age stood. She stood the way she had always stood, with the directness of a woman who had spent seven decades saying what she meant in this community and had no plans to stop.

She turned and looked at the collaborator.

"Honey," she said. "There is not a single parent in this room who would have done one thing differently than you did."

She sat back down.

The room was quiet for a moment. Then something moved through it that was not quite sound and not quite movement but was both, the specific collective exhale of two hundred people who had been holding something and had just been given permission to set it down.

Earl Hendricks said from the third row, without standing, "The child was alive the whole time?"

"Yes," James said. "She's home and she's recovering."

Earl nodded. "Good." He looked at the collaborator with the steady assessment of a man who had been farming through difficult seasons for fifty years. "You did what any one of us would have done," he said. "Don't let anybody tell you different."

Tom Hargrove said, from the second row, "The generator and the smokehouse. Those are losses we absorb together. That's what we do." He said it with the flat certainty of a man stating a fact rather than offering an opinion. "We don't go looking for someone to blame inside these walls when the people responsible are outside them."

Bill Miller, who had said nothing from the front row, said without standing: "They used my creek drainage to get to my property. I've been wondering about that for weeks." He paused. "Now I know." He looked at the collaborator. "My family's safe. Your daughter's safe. That's what matters."

The collaborator's face was doing something complicated. James watched it from the front of the room and understood what he was watching, which was a person who had been carrying something alone for three weeks and who was now having the weight of it taken from their hands by their neighbors and was not yet sure what to do with their hands now that they were empty.

Gary Whitfield spoke from the back. He had been in the grain facility that Thursday night. "I know what it cost to get her back," he said. "I was there." He paused. "I also know what I would have done if it was my kid. Every person in this room knows what they would have done."

Nobody argued with that. There was nothing to argue with because it was simply true and everyone in the room knew it was true.

Danny McClanahan, who had been sitting near the back with his arms crossed since before James started speaking, uncrossed them.

Patricia Ashcraft stood from the front row. She had her legal pad but she had not written anything on it. "I want to talk about the people who put this family in that position," she said. "Because that is where my anger is and I suspect I'm not alone."

She was not alone. The room confirmed it immediately through the specific quality of two hundred people shifting their attention in the same direction simultaneously.

"A family in this community was targeted deliberately," Patricia said. "A child was taken deliberately. The people who did that understood exactly what they were doing and exactly what it would cost the family they chose. They chose it anyway." She looked at James. "I want to know what we can do about that."

James told her. What Reeves had on the four men recovered from the facility. The two who were still unaccounted for. The organization behind them that was larger than what they had directly encountered and that was not going to stop because one operation had been disrupted. The steps he was taking to harden the community's security.

He told her plainly and without softening it because Patricia Ashcraft had never needed anything softened and because the room deserved the honest version.

When he finished Patricia sat down and made a note on her legal pad for the first time since the meeting started.

Sarah McClanahan, who had come from the diner and was standing along the wall, said: "What does this family need from us right now?"

The question landed in the room and did its own work. Immediate and specific and entirely characteristic of Sarah McClanahan, who had been feeding this community through its crisis for six weeks and whose instinct in every difficult moment was to ask what needed to be done and then do it.

Several people answered simultaneously. James let them talk.

***

The conversation that followed lasted an hour.

Not the difficult grinding conversation James had prepared himself for. Something warmer and more purposeful. People talking about what the family needed and what the community could provide and how to make sure that what had happened to them did not happen to anyone else.

There were moments of difficulty. Gerald Park said honestly that he needed some time to work through his feelings about the watch position information that had been compromised and that he was not yet where some of the others in the room were but that he was working on it. The room received that honestly too. Nobody demanded more from him than he had. Ruth Saylor told him that was fine and that time was something they all had plenty of at the moment.

The collaborator spoke once, near the end of the hour.

They stood up and looked at the room and said: "I know what it cost. I know what I did. I'm going to spend however long it takes making it right. Not because I was asked to. Because this is my home and these are my people and there is no other way I know how to live in this town."

They sat back down.

The room was quiet for a moment.

Then Margaret Hendricks, who had been sitting in the front row through the entire meeting without her information table and without the organized calm she normally brought to public situations, stood up and walked to the middle of the hall and sat down next to the collaborator and took their hand.

She did not say anything.

She did not need to.

***

The meeting ended at one-fifteen in the afternoon.

People filed out with the particular quality of a group that had done something together and knew it. The specific quality of a community that had been tested and had responded the way it had been responding for six weeks, by being what it was.

James stayed until the hall was empty except for Margaret Hendricks, still sitting with the collaborator, talking quietly in the way that two people talked when one of them had been through something hard and the other had known them long enough to know what they needed to hear.

He went outside and stood on the Carnegie Hall steps and looked at Main Street.

Moores Hill was still standing.

He went back inside to finish the day's work.

There was always more work to do.

CHAPTER 19: THE RESPONSE

The letter came on a Tuesday morning in the tenth week.

Emma knew it was different before she opened it.

Not from the outside. The envelope was the same paper as the previous correspondence, the slightly heavier stock with the particular texture she had come to recognize as belonging to this family and this country and this specific quality of careful communication. Her Carnegie Hall address in the same deliberate handwriting. The same post office box return address with no city or country named.

What was different was the weight of it.

She had been checking Gerald Sims's incoming stack every Tuesday and Friday since the first letter arrived. She had learned over those weeks the specific physical grammar of correspondence, the way an envelope communicated something about its contents before it was opened, the density of paper inside, the way it sat in the hand. This envelope sat differently than the others. Fuller. The particular weight of something that had been carefully considered before being committed to paper, the weight not just of pages but of the time that had gone into them.

She thanked Gerald and put it in her bag and walked to Carnegie Hall.

She did not open it there. She went to her east window table and set it in front of her and sat with it for a moment the way she sat with things that required her full attention before she gave them that attention, the particular discipline of someone who had learned that the quality of receiving something important was as important as the something itself.

Rufus settled under the table. His chin on her foot. His weight the familiar anchor it always was.

She opened the envelope.

***

The letter was eight pages.

She had never received eight pages from them before. The previous letters had been four pages at most, thorough and considered but bounded, the correspondence of people who were careful with what they committed to paper and who had been cautious in the early exchanges about how much to offer before they understood who they were offering it to.

This letter was different from the first line.

It began not with the formal acknowledgment she had come to expect but with something more direct, the opening of people who had made a decision about the person they were writing to and were no longer holding anything back. They addressed her by her first name. They had not done that before.

She read slowly.

The first section was about the network. The full picture of it, more complete than anything they had shared in the previous correspondence, the specific history of the seven sites and the custodian families as the English family understood it from a vantage point of several centuries of documented transmission. Things Emma had not known. Details that crossed and confirmed and expanded what she had found in Robert Moore's journals and the Carnegie Hall basement and the box that Patricia Ashcraft had carried in a closet for thirty years.

She read that section twice, stopping to write in her custodian notebook, cross-referencing against what she already knew, feeling the specific satisfaction of a picture becoming more complete with each new piece added to it. The Stonehenge site and its relationship to the Carnegie Hall site was described in terms she had not had before, the specific complementary nature of the two, the way they had been designed to function in relation to each other across the distance of an ocean in a way that neither could achieve independently. She wrote three pages of notes in the shorthand she had been developing for three months, the private notation of an investigation that had become something larger than any investigation she had originally intended to conduct.

When she finished writing she sat for a moment with her pen in her hand and looked at what she had.

Then the letter turned.

She felt it before she registered it consciously, the specific quality of a text shifting its register, moving from the transmission of information to something that required a different kind of attention. The sentence structure changed. The particular formality that had characterized every previous letter from this family relaxed into something more personal and she felt the relaxation as a physical thing, the way you felt a room temperature change when you moved from one space to another.

They wrote about a man.

Not by name. They were careful about that, the same carefulness with which they had been careful about everything, the particular discretion of people who understood that letters traveled through hands they did not control and that some things were not theirs to name in writing. But they wrote about him in a way that left no space for uncertainty about who they were describing.

A man who had come to them. Not recently. Years ago.

Emma set her pen down.

She had known this moment was coming. She had been building toward it for three months through estate records and a retired lawyer's office files and a retirement community in Kentucky and two names written in her custodian notebook with single underlines. She had told herself she was ready for it.

She understood, reading the first sentence about this man, that she had not been ready for it.

There was a difference between knowing something intellectually and receiving it through eight pages of careful handwriting from people who had known him for longer than she had known he was alive.

She made herself continue reading.

They described his arrival. The condition of him when he came, not the comfortable American with resources that she might have imagined, but someone worn by what he had been through to get there and by the decision that had brought him there in the first place. They described the quality of his knowledge, the specific things he knew that could only have come from the custodian lineage, presented without theater or performance, simply as what he had and what he was offering as the basis on which he hoped to be received. They described their own initial uncertainty and the process by which that uncertainty had resolved itself, not through any declaration he made but through the accumulated evidence of who he was over time.

Emma read about who he had been when he arrived and felt the specific distance of twenty-three years collapsing in a way she had not prepared for.

She had been eight years old when he left. She had a child's memories of him, the specific fragmentary quality of early childhood memory, impressions rather than coherent sequences. The smell of his workshirt. The way he laughed at something on the television in the evenings. The particular weight of his hand on the top of her head when she stood beside him. She had constructed a picture of him over the years from those fragments the way you constructed something from pieces that were too small to fully define the thing they came from, the picture incomplete and probably wrong in specific ways she could not identify because she had nothing to measure it against.

Now she had something to measure it against.

She read about the work he had contributed over the years. The infrastructure he had built, not the digital monitoring architecture she had found traces of in the databases but the physical and relational infrastructure of a custodian network that had been losing coherence for generations and that he had been quietly working to restore from the outside in. The relationships he had built with the other families. The way he had shared what he knew while also learning what they knew in a genuine exchange that had produced something neither side had before he arrived.

She read about the specific quality of his attention. The family described it in a way that made her stop reading and look at the table in front of her for a moment because the quality they described was one she recognized not from any memory of him but from her own experience of herself, the way she was aware of things in a room, the way she processed information, the specific analytical patience that she had always understood as characteristic of herself and that she was now reading described in someone else in terms that made it unmistakable.

She had her father's mind.

She had not known that before. She had known it as her own mind, simply as the way she thought, and now she was reading it described in a man she had not seen in twenty-three years and understanding something about herself that she had not had the information to understand before.

She set the letter down on the table and looked at Carnegie Hall's east windows for a moment. At Main Street beyond them going about its Tuesday morning. At the bell tower visible against the sky.

Then she picked the letter up and kept reading.

They wrote about who he had become over the years in their community. Not the arrival but the accumulation. The specific texture of a person who had been living and working in the same place among the same people for a long time and who had become, in that time, something that was inseparable from the community around him. The relationships. The trust that had been built not through declarations but through the consistent evidence of behavior over many years. The particular way he was present with people, the quality of attention he brought to conversations, the specific way he listened that the family described in a single phrase that Emma read three times.

He listens as if what you are saying is the most important thing he has heard.

She thought about what it meant to carry that quality through twenty-three years of separation from the people he had left. What it cost. What it meant that he had given that quality to this community, to these people, fully and without reservation, while carrying the weight of what he had left behind.

She thought about her mother. About what Linda Caldwell had carried through thirty-plus years of protecting Carnegie Hall without knowing the full scope of why, sustained by the instinct that it needed protecting. About what it meant that two people who had loved each other and built a life together had each spent the rest of their lives in service to the same thing without knowing the other was doing it.

She did not let herself stay with that thought long. Not yet. It was too large and she was still reading and the letter had not finished.

***

The shift came gradually and then suddenly.

They moved from description to disclosure with the specific quality of people who had been building toward something and had arrived at it. They wrote that her letter had been received and read.

Not by them alone.

Emma stopped.

She read that sentence again.

They wrote that a man who read their correspondence had read her letter. That he had been present when it arrived, as he often was, and that he had read it alongside them as he sometimes did when the correspondence concerned matters he was connected to.

That he had read her letter.

That he had sat with it for three days without speaking about it.

That on the third day he had come to them and had asked, with the particular careful quality of someone who had been thinking about the exact right way to phrase a question for seventy-two hours, whether they would include something in their reply.

They had said yes.

Emma looked at the remaining pages of the letter in her hand.

She turned to the last page of the family's letter.

Folded inside it, separately, a single piece of paper. Smaller than the letter pages. A different paper entirely, not the family's careful stock but something plainer, the kind of paper a person reached for when they needed to write something they had not planned to write and did not have the right materials available and used what was at hand because the writing could not wait for the right materials.

The handwriting was different from the family's deliberate script.

It was a man's handwriting. The specific quality of someone who had learned to write in a particular era and in a particular way that was neither elegant nor careless but that had the legibility of someone who wrote things down because the things mattered and wanted them to be read correctly.

She had never seen this handwriting before.

She recognized it the way you recognized something that had been part of you before you had words for recognition. Not memory. Something older than memory. The specific quality of encountering something that your body understood before your mind caught up to what your body was telling you.

She read the six sentences.

She read them again.

She set the letter down on the table.

Rufus shifted under the table. He moved from his position beneath her feet and came around beside her and pressed himself against her leg with the full weight of his body, the specific quality of presence he offered when presence was the only thing available and the only thing required. Not the alert attentive presence of a dog monitoring a situation. Something quieter than that. The presence of an animal who understood that the person beside him needed to not be alone and who had decided, without deliberation, that he would be the thing that made that true.

Emma put her hand on him and sat there for a long time with the six sentences on the table in front of her and Carnegie Hall's stone walls around her holding the particular coolness that 1907 construction held through the summer heat.

Outside the east windows Main Street went about its Tuesday morning. The community that had been managing its crisis for ten weeks moving through its adapted routines with the quiet efficiency of people who had found their rhythm inside a difficult reality and were living inside it without apology.

Rufus pressed against her and she put her face in her hands and sat there in the east window of Carnegie Hall with the six sentences her father had written on the table in front of her and the dark bell tower outside the window and the world going about its business around her, unchanged, unaware, exactly as it had been before the letter arrived.

We do not show you what they say.

Not yet.

Some things belong to Emma first.

CHAPTER 20: THE SLOW GRIND

The weeks after the tenth blurred into each other in a way the earlier weeks had not.

James had anticipated this. The first weeks of the outage had run on the particular fuel of shock and urgency, the specific energy of people who had been confronted with something they had never encountered and who were moving through it on the biochemistry of emergency. That fuel was not sustainable. It was designed to get human beings through the immediate danger and into a position from which the slower work of survival could begin.

The slower work was harder.

The watch rotation was established and running. The farm circuit was a known quantity. The resource inventory was being managed by people who understood it. The daily briefings had settled into a rhythm the community could navigate without the quality of anxious attention the first weeks had required. By every measurable standard Moores Hill was functioning better in week twelve than it had been in week two.

What was harder was the absence of urgency to sustain the effort. When the immediate urgency faded and the work continued anyway the work had to be chosen every day, actively, against the particular weight of exhaustion that accumulated in a body and a mind that had been operating at elevated capacity for months without adequate rest.

James watched it in the people around him. Not failure. A specific kind of wearing that showed in small ways. The slight drag in people's movements by afternoon. The shorter tempers in situations that would have been absorbed without friction in the first weeks. The quality of laughter that had changed, still present, still genuine, but requiring more to produce.

He started his briefings fifteen minutes earlier to give people more evening time at home. He did not announce it or explain it. He simply moved the briefing time and the community adapted within two days.

He drove the perimeter circuit every evening and noticed the specific changes that weeks of pressure produced in familiar ground. The farms looked different in August than they had in June. The summer harvest beginning without the equipment that normally ran it, by hand and by animal, the fields worked and productive but carrying the evidence of the effort it had taken to make them that way.

He stopped at the Hendricks farm on a Tuesday evening in the thirteenth week and sat on the porch with Earl and looked at the fields in the late August light and did not say anything for a while.

"How much longer?" Earl said finally. Not with impatience. With the plain honest curiosity of a man who was managing a calculation and needed a variable he did not currently have.

"I don't know," James said. "The shortwave operators are hearing things that suggest the restoration work is moving faster than initial estimates. But I don't have a date."

Earl looked at his fields. "We'll manage," he said. It was not optimism. It was assessment. The flat honest accounting of a man who knew exactly what he had and what it would take and had done the arithmetic.

James believed him.

He drove back to Moores Hill in the dark and thought about what it meant that Earl Hendricks's we'll manage was the most stabilizing thing he had heard in three weeks.

***

The fuller picture of what had happened at St. Leon came in pieces over weeks eleven and twelve.

Through the shortwave operators and the travelers on the county roads, bits of it arriving over the course of those weeks, each one adding detail to a picture that was already understood in its outline but that kept acquiring texture as the people who had been part of it found words for what they had experienced.

The casualty numbers were worse than the fragments James had reported at the briefing where he first told the community about it. What came in over the following weeks was more specific and sobering. The Battle of St. Leon, as it was being called now across the region, had been one of the most significant confrontations between civilians that southern Indiana had ever seen.

He presented the updated information at a town meeting in week twelve.

He told them what he knew. The fuller count. The specific nature of what the St. Leon defenders had faced and what they had done and what it had cost. He told them about Karl Schuman and Mark Andres and the families who had come from Dover and New Alsace and Yorkville and who had stood on SR 1 above I-74 with school buses and farming tools and whatever improvised capability four communities could assemble in thirty-six hours.

Earl Hendricks said from the third row, after James finished, "That could have been US 350."

"Yes," James said. "It could have been."

"Because of the overpass," Earl said. It was not a question. He was doing the geography in his head, US 350 running through the center of Moores Hill, the community's vulnerability from the east.

"The geography is different," James said. "Our approach from the west doesn't have the same natural chokepoint that the St. Leon exit provided. Which is why what Karl Schuman did with that overpass was as effective as it was. He had the right ground." He paused. "We've been thinking about what the right ground is for Moores Hill. The answer isn't one place. It's multiple places and multiple layers."

He told the community about it now. Not all the details. The outline of it, enough to understand that the response to what had happened at St. Leon was not to feel fortunate that it had happened elsewhere but to prepare for the possibility that the conditions that produced it were not unique to one exit on one highway.

Patricia Ashcraft asked three specific questions about the defensive architecture. James answered all three. She made notes. The meeting ended.

People filed out into the August night and went home to their houses and the particular rhythms of life inside an extended outage that were by now so familiar as to require no conscious thought.

***

The weeks between twelve and fifteen moved with the specific quality of time that has become routine.

Not comfortable. Not easy. Routine in the sense that the shape of each day was known before it began and could be moved through without the energy expenditure that novelty required.

Moores Hill had internalized the work of its own survival.

The watch rotation ran without the reminders it had required in the first weeks. The farm circuit happened twice a day with Danny McClanahan at the wheel with the reliability of someone who had done something so many times that the question of whether to do it had stopped arising. The community briefings had shortened as the material became more familiar, the daily reports becoming the kind of information that required acknowledgment rather than processing.

Carnegie Hall remained the community's center of gravity, but the quality of the gathering had changed. People came not because they needed information or direction but because they needed the particular comfort of a shared space where the shared experience of the past months was present and acknowledged without having to be discussed. Margaret Hendricks's information table had become something more like a community hearth.

James found himself at Carnegie Hall more than his operational requirements demanded.

He did not examine this too closely.

By September the days were shortening in the particular way of Indiana September, the summer heat still present but the light shifting, the angle of the sun dropping slightly each day toward something that would eventually be winter. The farms were deep into harvest work, the fall crops coming in with the same improvised human effort as the summer crops but with the additional pressure of timing, the knowledge that harvest had a window and that the window did not adjust itself for the absence of equipment.

James drove the farm circuit himself in the third week of September to give Danny McClanahan three days off. Not because Danny asked. Because James had been watching Danny for four months and understood that the particular kind of tiredness Danny was carrying was the kind that needed rest rather than will.

Danny protested once and then accepted it with the grace of someone who was tired enough to know he needed it.

***

Mr. Patterson was on his porch on a cool September morning when James drove past on his early circuit.

James stopped.

Patterson was sitting in his chair with his thermos mug, the same chair and the same thermos mug he had been in on the first morning of the outage, with the particular composed patience of a man who had outlasted every difficult thing the world had thrown at him and expected to outlast this one too.

"Morning James," Patterson said.

"Morning," James said through the truck window.

"Getting cooler," Patterson said. He said it the way he said everything, as a plain statement of observable fact, without complaint or concern.

"Yes," James said. "It is."

Patterson looked at the dark porch light above his head. The one he had told James he left on for his wife. He had been leaving it switched on every evening since the first day of the outage, the switch in the on position even though the bulb had been dark for four months, the particular habit of grief that did not require electricity to maintain itself.

"You think it'll be back before winter sets in hard?" Patterson said.

"I think so," James said. "I think it'll be close."

Patterson nodded. Drank from his thermos. "Good," he said. "I'd like to see that light on again before it gets too cold to sit out here."

James drove the rest of his circuit with that in mind.

***

The announcement about the appliances arrived on a Thursday morning in the fifteenth week through Roy Simmons's shortwave.

Roy had been the communication relay from his house since week one, the bad knee and the three grandchildren having kept him out of the physical watch rotation and into the role that suited him better, the patient methodical monitoring of the shortwave frequencies where official and semi-official communications traveled in the absence of functional broadcast infrastructure.

He called James on the two-way immediately.

The announcement had come through a FEMA frequency, official language, clearly prepared and distributed widely because Roy reported that he had already heard it on three separate frequencies by the time he reached James. It was addressed to all citizens in the affected grid restoration zone and the thing James wrote in his notebook and then went directly to Carnegie Hall to share was this.

Do not assume restoration will come with warning. When grid power returns to your area it may do so without advance notice and at any hour. Before restoration occurs all citizens should unplug or power off all electrical appliances, devices, and systems in their homes and businesses. Failure to do so risks fire hazards and equipment damage from power surges that accompany initial restoration. Repeat: unplug everything before the grid returns.

He read it at the briefing that evening and watched the room process the specific thing the announcement meant, which was that the grid was coming back. Not tomorrow. Not next week necessarily. But coming back, in the near enough future that the federal agency responsible for managing the restoration was now communicating proactively about how to receive it safely.

The mood in the briefing room shifted in a way that James had not seen in months.

Not celebration. Not the dramatic relief he might have expected. Something quieter and more complicated, the specific emotional register of people who had been living inside a very long difficult thing and who had just been told, with the authority of an official government communication, that the very long difficult thing was going to end.

Margaret Hendricks asked how long.

James said he did not know but that the fact of the announcement suggested weeks rather than months.

She nodded. Wrote something on her notepad.

The meeting ended earlier than usual that night. Not because there was less to cover. Because the room needed to go home and sit with the news in private, each person in their own house with their own family, doing the specific human work of allowing themselves to believe that something difficult was coming to an end.

James drove the perimeter circuit afterward in the early October dark and thought about the announcement and what it meant and what the return of the grid would require from a community that had reorganized itself completely around its absence.

He thought about Mr. Patterson's porch light.

He thought it would be on before the first frost.

***

Emma had been writing the letter to her father for five weeks.

Not continuously. In the way that writing a difficult thing got written, returning to it when she had something new to say and setting it aside when she did not and never forcing it because the forcing produced something that sounded like what she wanted to say and was not actually what she wanted to say.

She wrote by candlelight at the kitchen table in the house where she grew up, the custodian notebook open in front of her, drafts accumulating in the pages behind the current working section. Each draft getting closer. Each one discarding something the previous one had been holding onto that did not belong, the way revision always worked when the writer was honest enough to recognize what was theirs and what was performance.

She had written about Montana. About the ceremony and what she had seen in the circle and the choice she had made there. She had written about Carnegie Hall and the inscription in the basement and what it meant to be the custodian of something that had been nearly lost. She had written about the ghost pattern and what it meant and following it through Marsh and Forsythe and the financial architecture to the conclusion that had been waiting at the end of the thread for twenty-three years.

She had written about reading his six sentences.

That section she had written and discarded three times. The first two versions were too careful, the emotional truth of them managed into language that was accurate but not honest. The third version was honest and frightened her slightly when she read it back, and she had set it aside for a week and come back to it and found that it was still right.

She kept it.

What she had not yet written was the ending.

Not because she did not know what it needed to say. She had known since the second week after the letter arrived, in the specific way that you knew things that had not yet arrived at the surface of consciousness but that were present underneath it, waiting for the conditions that would allow them to come up.

She thought about what she wanted to say to him before the tools came back. Before the world changed again and the particular quality of the weeks since his letter arrived was replaced by something else.

She picked up her pen.

She wrote the ending.

It was not long. It did not need to be long. It said what it said in the specific language of someone who had been raised by a woman who protected things without always knowing why and who had inherited that quality and who was now using it to protect something she had not yet decided how to name.

She read it back.

She kept it.

Outside the kitchen window Carnegie Hall's bell tower stood in the dark the way it had stood in the dark for four months. Permanent. Present. Exactly where it had always been whether the lights were on or not.

Emma closed the custodian notebook and went to bed.

Tomorrow she would copy the letter cleanly and take it to Gerald Sims.

The grid would come back when it came back.

Until then there was still work to do.

CHAPTER 21: THE LONG WAY DOWN

The grid came back to Moores Hill on a Tuesday and James spent the days that followed watching the community's reaction with the careful attention he brought to everything that mattered.

Not celebration. Not relief, or not only relief. Something more complicated than either of those things, the specific emotional state of people who had been holding something at maximum tension for four months and were now being told they could let go, and who were discovering that letting go was its own kind of work.

The first hours had a quality he had not expected. He had anticipated noise, the particular social noise of a community releasing pressure, voices in the street and doors opening and people finding each other to confirm that yes, the lights were on, yes, the refrigerators were running, yes, it was real. What he got instead was a strange quiet. People stepping onto their porches and standing there looking at their lit windows as if the light needed to be confirmed from the outside before it could be fully believed. Children who were newborns before the outage, who had no memory of powered life, looking at the overhead lights in their kitchens with the specific wonder of encountering something for the first time that everyone around them was treating as a return.

Mr. Patterson was on his porch next door to Emma's house when the grid came back, as he had been on his porch on the first morning of the outage. James drove past on his circuit and saw him there and stopped.

Patterson was looking at his porch light. The one that had been dark since June. He had turned it on when the power came back and was looking at it with an expression James had not seen on his face in four months, which was the expression of someone who had not fully realized how much they had missed something until they had it back.

"Seventy-three years," Patterson said when James stopped beside his truck window.

"Sir?" James said.

"Lived in this house seventy-three years," Patterson said. "Never went more than three days without electricity." He looked at the porch light. "Four months is a long time."

"Yes," James said. "It is."

Patterson sat with that for a moment. "Think it'll hold this time?"

"The engineers say it will," James said. "The infrastructure work they've done is more substantial than what was there before."

"That's good," Patterson said. He looked at the light again. "My wife used to leave that light on for me when I worked late. Thirty years she did that." He was quiet. "She's been gone eleven years. I leave it on for myself now." He paused. "I missed that light."

James drove the rest of his circuit with that conversation in his mind.

***

By the second day the quiet had given way to something else.

He had anticipated this too, though not the specific form it took. He had expected the decompression to manifest as conflict, the grievances set aside for four months reasserting themselves with compound interest now that there was room for them. What he saw instead in the first several days was something more like disorientation, the specific unsteadiness of people who had reorganized their entire lives around the conditions of the crisis and were now having those conditions removed and were not entirely sure what to do with the space the removal left.

Tom Hargrove opened the hardware store to full operation on Friday morning and stood behind his counter in the particular way he always stood behind his counter and was visited by more customers in the first hour than he had served in the previous week, not because people needed hardware but because the hardware store being open in the normal way was a signal that things were returning to normal and people needed to stand in that signal for a few minutes and feel it.

Gerald Sims at the post office received seventeen people asking to collect their incoming mail before ten in the morning, people who had been receiving mail through the community collection system for four months and who now wanted to receive it the old way, at the window, from Gerald's hand, the particular ritual of normal postal operations that they had not known they valued until it was gone.

Sarah McClanahan's diner ran on grid power for the first time since June and Sarah served breakfast and lunch to more people than she had served on any single day of the outage, not because people were especially hungry but because the diner being open and running the way it had always run was another signal and people needed to be in the presence of that signal too.

James watched all of this from the particular vantage point of someone who had been moving through Moores Hill twice a day for four months and who understood the community's patterns well enough to read the deviations from them.

What he was watching for was not the obvious things. The obvious things, the arguments that seemed disproportionate to their subject, the grievances surfacing with compound interest, the resource allocation disputes that he had warned Patricia Ashcraft about, those would come and when they came he would manage them. He was watching for the subtler thing, the particular quality of people who had been through something significant together and were now processing it individually, each in their own way, at their own pace, in the privacy of their own households, and who needed to be seen in that processing without being managed or directed or told how to feel about what they had been through.

He had learned this from his years in law enforcement. The thing a community needed most in the aftermath of something significant was not solutions. It was witnesses. People whose job it was to see what had happened and to confirm that it had been real and that it had been hard and that the people who had been through it had done what they needed to do.

He made himself available for that role in the days after the grid restored.

He was not, by nature, a man given to extended conversation about feelings. He was a man given to action, to the practical business of identifying problems and addressing them, and the part of himself that wanted to identify the problem of community decompression and address it through a specific program of organized activities had to be managed carefully. The community did not need a program. It needed time and presence and the knowledge that the person who had been managing their crisis was still paying attention.

He paid attention.

He had anticipated this. He had read enough about disaster recovery in the years before the outage, in the professional development reading that law enforcement did and that most people did not know law enforcement did, to understand that the period immediately following a sustained crisis was its own category of vulnerability. Communities that held together under pressure sometimes fractured when the pressure released. The shared purpose that had organized everything for four months dissolved and the individual purposes underneath it, which had been present all along but subordinated to the collective need, reasserted themselves with an intensity proportional to how long they had been suppressed.

The grid coming back did not mean the crisis was over. It meant the nature of the crisis had changed.

He had told Patricia Ashcraft this the morning after the grid restored. She had listened with the legal pad on her knee and the pen in her hand and had not written anything down, which was how he knew she was receiving something she considered important rather than something she was cataloguing.

"What does it look like?" she said. "When communities fracture coming out of a crisis."

"It looks like arguments that seem disproportionate to what they're about," he said. "People who held it together through the hard part finding reasons to be angry at each other once the hard part is over. Grievances that were set aside for the duration coming back with compound interest."

Patricia looked at her legal pad. "The collaborator situation."

"Yes," James said. "And other things."

"What other things?"

"Decisions that were made collectively in the crisis that individuals had reservations about. Resource allocation that people accepted because they had to and will now revisit because they can. The watch rotation and who carried what load. The farm circuit and what it cost the people who ran it." He paused. "People who lost things. The Kowalski smokehouse. The Miller generator. Losses that were absorbed during the crisis without being processed because there wasn't time or space to process them."

Patricia was quiet for a moment. "How long does this period last?"

"Depends on the community," James said. "And on whether it's managed or left to run."

She looked at him. "Manage it."

***

He started with the people who had carried the most weight.

Not the people who had held public roles. Margaret Hendricks and Gerald Sims and Tom Hargrove had been visible throughout and the community had been watching them and would continue to watch them and their transitions would happen under observation that provided its own kind of structure. He was thinking about the people who had carried invisible weight, the weight that did not show up in the daily briefings or the community resource inventory or any of the documentation that the crisis had produced.

Danny McClanahan had driven the farm circuit twice a day for four months. He had driven the mail run to Lawrenceburg and back in an armored truck through roads that had gotten progressively more difficult. He had been the driver the night they brought the girl home from the grain facility. James went to his house on the Saturday after the grid restored and sat with him on the porch for two hours and they talked about nothing in particular, which was the right conversation for that specific moment.

Carol Beatty had been the medical infrastructure for Moores Hill through four months of a crisis that had no functional healthcare system behind it. She had treated injuries and illnesses and the specific psychological presentations of people who had been under sustained stress for longer than human beings were designed for. She had treated the girl from the grain facility. She had been at the Legion in St. Leon, information had since confirmed, though she had not told anyone because that was Carol Beatty and she did not talk about the things she did. James went to her house and told her that he knew and that it mattered and that Moores Hill owed her something it was probably not capable of fully paying.

She told him to stop being dramatic.

He told her she was welcome.

Gary Whitfield had been on the grain facility operation and had been managing watch rotation personnel for four months with the particular invisible competence of someone who made difficult things look straightforward. James found him at his house splitting wood, the same as the first time, and this time James picked up the second maul from the rack and split wood beside him for an hour without either of them saying much and that was also the right conversation for that specific moment.

He talked to Sarah McClanahan at the diner on a Tuesday morning.

The diner was running on grid power now, the propane setup that had kept it functioning through four months still there, still operational, now supplemented by the returning electricity rather than operating in its absence. Sarah was behind the counter doing what Sarah always did, which was feeding people with the efficient calm of someone who had found the thing they were suited for and was doing it without drama or expectation.

He sat at the counter and she put coffee in front of him without being asked and he looked at her for a moment.

"How are you?" he said.

She looked at him with the specific expression of a sister who had known her brother for thirty-four years and understood exactly what he was actually asking. "I'm fine James," she said. "I'm more worried about you than about me."

"Don't be," he said.

"That's exactly what someone I should be worried about would say," she said.

He drank his coffee. She refilled it. The diner went about its morning around them with the particular quality of a place that had been through something significant and was finding its way back to what it was, not quite the same as before but recognizably itself.

"Owen's doing well," Sarah said. Not casually. With the specific quality of information offered to someone who she thought needed to hear it.

"I know," James said. "I've seen him."

"He's writing," Sarah said. "About what happened out there. On the road."

James thought about Owen Mitchell riding a mule from Colorado to Indiana through a country that had been through something that would take years to fully understand. About what Owen had seen on those roads and what he had done to get home and what he was now making of it in the particular way that former investigative reporters made things of what they had witnessed.

"Good," James said. "It should be written."

Sarah refilled his coffee a second time and they sat together in the comfortable silence of being siblings, of two people who had known each other their whole lives and did not need to fill every moment with words.

***

He found Emma at Carnegie Hall on a Wednesday afternoon.

She had been there every day since the grid restored, at the east window table, working with the particular focused intensity of someone who had been waiting for their tools to come back and was now using them with the urgency of four months of accumulated waiting behind each search. He had watched her from a distance, not intrusively, the way he watched everything that mattered to him, with attention that was present without being intrusive.

She was different since the letter had arrived. He had noticed it the day she came back from Gerald Sims's window with the envelope that sat differently in her hand than the previous ones. He had seen it in the specific quality of her stillness in the days after she opened it, the particular internal quality of someone who had received something significant and was doing the slow work of integrating it.

He had not asked.

He sat down across from her now at the east window table in the afternoon light with the grid running and the building's systems functioning for the first time in four months and the particular quality of Carnegie Hall in full electrical operation, the lights and the security system and the faint hum of infrastructure that the building had been making his whole life without him consciously registering it.

Emma looked up from her laptop.

She looked at him for a moment with the expression of someone who has been deciding whether to say something for a long time and has just decided.

"James," she said.

"Yeah," he said.

"I need to tell you something."

He waited the way he waited for everything important. With the steady patience of someone who had learned that the significant things arrived on their own schedule and that the correct response to their arrival was to be present and still.

"My father is alive," Emma said.

The afternoon light came through the east windows at the angle it always came through them at this time of day in October, lower than the summer angle, the quality of it different, the particular light of a season that was moving toward its end.

James looked at her steadily.

"I know," he said.

Emma stopped.

She looked at him with the specific expression of someone who has just said the most significant thing they have said in a long time and has received a response that was not any of the responses they had prepared for.

"What?" she said.

"I've known since Kentucky," James said. "You went to see Forsythe and you came back different. I've been doing this work long enough to know what a person looks like when they've found what they were looking for and it's bigger than they expected."

Emma looked at him. "You didn't say anything."

"You weren't ready," James said. "There's a difference between knowing something and being ready to say it out loud. I wasn't going to ask you to do that before you were ready."

The sounds from Main Street filtered through the Carnegie Hall windows. The particular ambient sound of a town that had electricity again, the layered hum of it that was already becoming background noise the way it had been background noise before June and would be background noise again within a week because that was how human beings related to the infrastructure that sustained them.

"How much do you know?" Emma said.

"What I put together from watching," James said. "Not the details. The shape of it."

Emma looked at the custodian notebook on the table in front of her. At the months of accumulated investigation inside it, the estate records and the two names and the financial architecture and the letter from England and the six sentences she had not shown anyone.

She opened the notebook to the beginning of what she had been building and pushed it across the table to him.

"Read it," she said. "All of it. Then ask me whatever you want to ask."

James pulled the notebook toward him.

He read with the focused complete attention he brought to everything that required it, not skimming, not summarizing as he went, reading the way he had always read evidence and documents and the accumulated record of an investigation, fully and in sequence and without reaching conclusions before the material was finished.

It took forty minutes.

When he finished he closed the notebook and pushed it back across the table and looked at Emma.

"What do you need?" he said.

Emma looked at him. At the notebook. At the east windows where Carnegie Hall's bell tower was visible against the October sky, the floodlights on it in the late afternoon the way they had always been on it before June and the way they were on it again now.

"I don't know yet," she said. "But I'm telling you anyway."

"Good," James said.

Neither of them reached for their coffee.

Emma looked at the custodian notebook on the table between them. At everything it contained and everything it had cost to build and everything that came next that neither of them could fully see yet.

Then she looked at James.

He was already looking at her.

She stood up from the table and he stood up from the table and they met in the middle of the east window of Carnegie Hall in the afternoon light and held on to each other the way people held on when they had been through something significant together and needed to confirm that the other person was still there and real and present.

Neither of them said anything.

There was nothing that needed to be said.

Outside the east windows Carnegie Hall's bell tower stood in the October light, the floodlights back on it for the first time in four months, permanent and present and exactly where it had always been. Main Street going about its afternoon. The grid running steadily through the wires that had been waiting for it.

Emma felt the tears before she was aware she had decided to cry. Not the dramatic tears of someone performing grief. The quiet unstoppable kind that arrived when the body finally had permission to release something it had been holding for a very long time.

She did not pull back. She did not apologize for them.

James held on.

After a while she felt something against her hair. The specific warmth of it. She understood without looking that James McClanahan, who had held everything together for four months without flinching, who had stood at the front of Carnegie Hall and told two hundred people the truth about hard things more times than she could count, who had carried his own weight and the community's weight simultaneously without complaint or ceremony, had a tear running down his face.

She held on tighter.

They stood together in the east window of Carnegie Hall for a long time. The afternoon light moving slowly across the floor around them. The bell tower outside. The town going about its business. The world that had been dark for four months finding its way back to function one street at a time.

When they finally stepped back from each other neither of them acknowledged what had just happened and both of them understood it completely.

James looked at her.

"Your mother would be proud of you," he said.

Emma looked at the bell tower outside the window.

"I know," she said quietly. "I think she already was."

She picked up the custodian notebook.

There was work to do.

CHAPTER 22: THE SEARCH

Emma sent the letter on a Wednesday morning.

Not the Tuesday she had planned. She had copied it out cleanly from the custodian notebook on Tuesday evening, the final version after five weeks of drafts, and had read it back once and had found one sentence that was not quite right, not wrong exactly but not right, not saying precisely what she meant in precisely the way she meant it, and she had set it aside and rewritten that sentence by candlelight and gone to bed and awoken with the specific clarity of someone who has slept on a decision and found it unchanged in the morning.

The sentence was right now.

She folded the letter and addressed the envelope to the post office box and walked to Gerald Sims's counter before eight in the morning. Gerald took it with the particular care he brought to every piece of outgoing correspondence since the early weeks of the outage, the deliberate handling of someone who understood that the physical object in his hand was the only version of the communication it contained and that there was no backup and no resend.

"International," Emma said.

"I'll make sure it goes out on today's run," Gerald said.

She thanked him and walked back to Carnegie Hall in the October morning with the particular quality of someone who has done a thing they have been building toward for a long time and who is now in the specific suspended state that follows completion, not relief exactly, not accomplishment exactly, something between the two that had no clean name.

She sat at her east window table.

The grid had been back for two weeks. The building's systems were running, the security system and the lights and the faint ambient hum of infrastructure that Carnegie Hall had been making her whole life. Her laptop was open. Her monitoring systems had been restarting and recalibrating since the grid came back, the particular sequence of a complex digital operation returning to function after an extended absence, each system finding its way back at its own pace.

She had been patient with the restart sequence. More patient than she would have been before the outage. Four months of working without the tools had produced in her a specific relationship with the tools that she had not had before, the relationship of someone who understood what it meant to be without them and who did not take their return for granted.

Rufus was under the table. His chin on her foot. His weight the familiar anchor.

She opened the monitoring dashboard and looked at the status of the seven sites.

***

The sites were clean.

All seven. Montana stable. Carnegie Hall stable. The active sites in Peru and England stable. Easter Island, Egypt, Turkey, all returning the same status they had been returning through the months of manual checking she had been doing through the physical records at Dorothy Webb's archive, the status of sites that were present and intact and not under active threat.

She documented the restart confirmation in her custodian notebook with the date and the specific status of each site, the same methodical documentation she had been maintaining since the beginning, the practice that the outage had not interrupted but had simply changed the medium of.

Then she ran the missing persons database search.

The seven site coordinates. The weekly search she had been running in digital form before the outage and by hand through the physical records during it. The search that had been her primary investigative tool for three months before the grid went down and that was now available to her again in its full digital form, with the speed and thoroughness that the digital version allowed.

She ran it and watched the results populate.

Clean. All clean. The same results the manual searches had been returning, confirming what she had already known but confirming it now with the full capability of the system rather than the partial picture that the physical records provided.

She sat back.

Then she ran the search for the ghost pattern.

***

It was a more complex search than the standard site monitoring. She had built it over three months before the outage, refining it through successive iterations until it was precise enough to catch the specific signatures of the monitoring infrastructure her father had been running without catching her own searches or the standard database queries that produced similar results.

She ran it and waited.

The traces were there. twenty years of them, exactly as she had found them in June before the grid went down, the specific fingerprint of a monitoring operation that had been running consistently and deliberately across the seven site coordinates for a decade and a half. The timestamps. The search patterns. The particular methodology of someone who knew exactly what they were looking for and had been looking for it the same way every week for twenty years.

She scrolled to the most recent entries.

The most recent timestamp was from June. The specific date in June, a Tuesday morning, the day the grid went down.

She checked the dates after it. Nothing. The search that had been running every week for twenty years had simply stopped. No degraded performance. No partial entries. No attempts that failed.

It had been running and then it had not been running and the line between the two was the exact date that the American Midwest grid had gone dark.

Her father had lost access the same morning she had.

He had not restarted.

She sat with that.

Not because she did not understand it. She understood it immediately and completely, the specific logic of it, a man in Peru with functioning international infrastructure who had watched the American grid failure unfold on the news the same morning it happened and who had understood immediately why his monitoring had gone dark and who had chosen, in the weeks and months since, not to restart it.

She thought about the letter she gave to Gerald Sims. About the five weeks of drafts and the sentence she had rewritten by candlelight. About the six sentences he had written that she had been carrying for five weeks.

She thought about what it meant that he had stopped monitoring.

Not what it meant in operational terms. She understood the operational terms. It meant the ghost pattern was gone and the sites were being maintained by the custodian families and by Emma herself and by the network she had been rebuilding and that did not require the external monitoring infrastructure he had built.

What she was sitting with was what it meant in the other terms. The personal terms. The terms that had nothing to do with the network and everything to do with a man who had built a monitoring system to watch over things he could not be present for and who had stopped running it.

She did not know yet what it meant. She wrote it in her custodian notebook and underlined it and left it as a question because it was a question and she was not in the habit of writing conclusions she had not reached.

She looked at the notebook for a long moment.

Then she opened a different database.

***

This was not the search she had planned to run.

She had been building toward the site monitoring restart and the ghost pattern check for two weeks, the specific sequence she had been planning since the grid came back and her tools had begun their restart. Those searches were complete. The notebook had the results. The next item on the investigative agenda was the correspondence with her father, the slow careful process of building something through letters that would eventually become what it was going to become.

But she was looking at the financial database with the account structures Forsythe had described in her notebook and something was pulling at her attention in the specific way that things pulled at her attention when the investigative instinct was recognizing a pattern before the conscious mind had caught up to what the pattern was.

She had learned to trust that pull. In three months of custodian investigation and before that in years of data security work, the pattern recognition that happened below the level of conscious thought had a better record than she was always comfortable admitting. It was not intuition in any mystical sense. It was the accumulated experience of someone who had spent a professional lifetime looking at systems, learning what healthy looked like, and developing the specific sensitivity to deviation that came from that accumulated familiarity.

Something was deviating.

She built the search carefully. It took forty minutes. She was working with the financial architecture Forsythe had documented in his kept copy, the account structures and routing patterns and specific signatures of her father's financial infrastructure, and she was building a query designed to find not the infrastructure itself but the connections adjacent to it. The things that touched it at specific points. The financial relationships between her father's accounts and other structures in the broader financial systems they moved through.

She ran it.

The results populated in three minutes.

She looked at them.

She looked at them again.

The financial architecture her father had built was there, the familiar structure of it, the layered accounts and the specific routing that Forsythe had described and that she had spent months understanding. She expected that. She had designed the search to find it as the baseline against which she was looking for something adjacent.

The adjacent thing was also there.

A financial connection she had not seen before. Not because it had not existed before. Because she had not been looking in this direction before, her searches focused on the custodian network and the seven sites and the question of her father's identity and presence. This connection ran parallel to the account structures her father had built but was not part of them. A separate architecture, connected at specific points through what appeared to be legitimate financial transactions but that produced, when traced through the connections Forsythe's documentation had made available to her, a pattern that was not legitimate.

She followed the thread.

The first connection was ambiguous. A financial transaction that could have been routine movement between legitimate accounts, the kind of thing that appeared in financial systems constantly and that required context to interpret. She noted it and moved to the next point in the chain.

The second connection was less ambiguous. The routing structure of it had a specific quality she recognized from her data security work, the particular architecture of a financial movement that was designed to obscure its origin and destination while maintaining the appearance of legitimate business. It was not crude. It was the work of someone who understood financial systems well enough to use them against their own transparency mechanisms.

She noted it and kept following.

The third connection stopped her.

Not because it was dramatically different from the first two. Because of where it led. The account it connected to was not in her father's network. It was not connected to the custodian families or the seven sites or any of the financial infrastructure she had been mapping for months. It was connected to something she had encountered before, in a different context, in the records from the investigation that had preceded her custodian work by nearly two years.

She recognized the signature.

She cross-referenced it against the Safety Coalition documentation she had built during the Carnegie Hall investigation. The specific financial fingerprints of an organization that had been operating for thirty years and that she had believed, until this moment, had been substantially neutralized by the events of the previous year.

Not neutralized. Reduced. The Moores Hill operation had been shut down. The people behind the local effort had been exposed and dealt with. But the Safety Coalition was not a local operation. It was thirty years old and it had infrastructure that predated Moores Hill and that had continued existing after Moores Hill the way a root system continued existing after a tree was cut down.

She was looking at part of that root system.

And it was connected, through a chain of financial relationships she could now trace in both directions, to the account structures her father had built in 2002.

She sat back from the laptop.

The particular stillness of someone who has just found something they were not looking for and who is doing the careful work of determining whether what they found is what it appears to be before they decide what it means.

She ran the trace again from the beginning. Slowly. Without the momentum of having already followed it once. Checking each step against the evidence rather than against her memory of the previous run, the specific discipline of someone who understood that the most dangerous investigative error was confirming what you already believed rather than following what the evidence actually showed.

The evidence showed the same thing it had shown the first time.

Someone had a financial connection to both the account structures her father had built and the surviving infrastructure of the Safety Coalition. Not a peripheral connection. Not a coincidental overlap in a shared financial system. A structural connection, deliberate and maintained, the kind that required active construction and ongoing management by someone who understood both architectures and had chosen to be present in both.

Someone who had a foot in both worlds.

Emma opened her custodian notebook to a fresh page.

She looked at the data on the screen. At the chain of connections she had traced. At the point where the two architectures met and the specific account that sat at that intersection.

The account had a registered administrator. A name attached to the structure in the way that financial accounts were required to have names attached to them regardless of how many layers of routing and misdirection surrounded them. The name was not one she recognized. It was not her father's name or either of the names in her notebook from the Marsh and Forsythe investigations.

It was a new name.

She wrote it in the custodian notebook.

She looked at it for a long moment. At the implications of it, which were significant and complicated and which she was not yet ready to fully trace because tracing them required the kind of thinking that needed to happen in conversation with someone else rather than alone at an east window table in Carnegie Hall in the October morning.

She underlined the name. Once.

She picked up her phone.

James answered on the second ring.

"James," she said.

"Yeah," he said.

"I need you to come to the east window table," she said. "Right now."

A pause. The specific quality of James McClanahan receiving a specific request from Emma Caldwell and calibrating it against everything he knew about both.

"On my way," he said.

Emma set the phone down and looked at the name in her notebook and looked at the east windows and Carnegie Hall's bell tower visible against the October sky and thought about what came next.

What came next was going to require everything Clue-Minati Investigative Services had.

She thought they were ready.

She thought, looking at the name in her notebook with its single underline, that they were going to have to be.

James's footsteps on the Carnegie Hall stairs.

Rufus lifted his head from Emma's foot and looked toward the door.

The Patron was waiting.

EPILOGUE

Two weeks later the world was still finding its way back.

Not all at once. Not cleanly. With the particular uneven quality of a system returning from significant damage, some parts faster than others, some parts not at all, the specific topology of recovery that reflected the specific topology of what had been lost and what had survived and what had been built in the absence of what was gone.

The stores were restocking. Not quickly. The supply chains that had been interrupted for four months did not restart in a day or a week and the particular gaps in what was available told the story of which supply chains had recovered and which had not. Tom Hargrove's hardware store had fasteners and hand tools and the basic inventory of a hardware store but the electrical components section was still largely empty, the specific items that the restoration work had consumed in enormous quantities not yet returned to the distribution system.

Sarah McClanahan's diner was running full service for the first time since June. Not because everything was available. Because Sarah McClanahan was not the kind of person who ran partial service when full service was possible and she had found the suppliers she needed and had made it work with the particular efficient determination that was simply who she was.

Emma ate breakfast there on a Tuesday morning and watched Main Street through the diner window and thought about what Moores Hill looked like now compared to what it had looked like in June and what it would look like in another four months and whether the two were the same town or different towns wearing the same name.

She thought they were the same town. Changed but the same. The way people were the same after something significant happened to them, carrying the evidence of what they had been through in ways that were not always visible but that were always present.

Owen was at the counter.

He had been at the counter most mornings since his return, the diner having become his primary working space in the weeks since the grid came back and his laptop had restarted and the book he was writing had accelerated from the notes and fragments he had been accumulating since he rode back into Moores Hill on a mule named Margaret to something that had the specific momentum of a project that had found its shape and was moving.

He had a publisher. Emma had learned this from Sarah rather than from Owen directly, which was characteristic of Owen, who did not announce things he considered still in progress and who considered everything in progress until it was finished. The publisher was interested in the road account, the specific story of what Owen had seen and done and survived between Telluride and the Oak Street moment that Emma was not going to let him write about in detail if she had any say in the matter.

She did not have any say in the matter.

Owen had told her this directly and without apology and with the particular quality of a former investigative reporter who understood that the story was the story and that personal comfort was not a factor in whether a true story got told.

Emma had told him she was going to read the manuscript before it went to the publisher.

Owen had told her she was welcome to read it after it went to the publisher.

The negotiation was ongoing.

Margaret the mule was at Earl Hendricks's farm, which was where Danny McClanahan had taken her the morning after Owen's return and where she had apparently decided to stay, having assessed the Hendricks property and its resources and its existing population of animals and concluded that it suited her. Earl had told Owen he was welcome to collect her at any time. Owen had told Earl he appreciated that. Neither of them had done anything further about it and Margaret had been at the Hendricks farm for three weeks and appeared to consider the matter settled.

***

The academic paper had been submitted.

Emma had learned this through Owen, who had learned it through channels she did not ask about because Owen's channels were Owen's channels and asking about them was not something she had ever found productive. Dr. Hanson's paper on the custodian network, the one that had been in development since before the outage and that the outage had delayed but not stopped, had been submitted to a peer review journal and was working its way through the process that academic papers worked through, slowly and without regard for the urgency anyone outside the process felt about the timeline.

Emma had mixed feelings about the paper.

Not about its existence. The academic documentation of the custodian network was something she had come to understand as necessary, the work of making the knowledge available in forms that survived the specific vulnerabilities of oral and personal transmission. What gave her the mixed feelings was the specific content of certain sections, the parts that were more accurate than she would have chosen to make them from an operational security perspective.

She had said this to Owen who had relayed it to Dr. Hanson who had made three specific adjustments that addressed the most significant of her concerns and had declined to make the others on the grounds that the accuracy of the record was the point of the record and that sanitizing it for operational security purposes defeated that point.

Emma had accepted this with the specific grace of someone who understood that they did not control everything and had decided to direct their energy toward the things they did control.

***

The Werner appeals were losing.

One by one, methodically, in the particular way that legal processes worked when the underlying case was sound and the appeals were being made from a position of diminishing options rather than genuine legal argument. James had been monitoring the proceedings through Reeves and through the county legal contacts that twelve years of law enforcement had built, and his read on the trajectory was that the appeals would exhaust themselves within the year and that the outcomes from the original proceedings would stand.

Emma noted this in her custodian notebook. Not as a closed item. As a development in an ongoing situation that had not yet fully resolved and that would require continued attention.

The Safety Coalition was not the Werner case. She had understood this since the beginning but the financial thread she had found in the databases three weeks ago had made it concrete in a way that the abstract understanding had not. The Werner case was a local operation, a specific attempt on a specific site by specific people who had been identified and dealt with. The Safety Coalition was thirty years old and it had survived the Werner case the way a root system survived the cutting of a branch.

She had told James everything the afternoon she found the name.

He had listened with the focused complete attention he brought to everything that required it and when she finished he had looked at the name in the notebook and asked two questions. The first was whether the financial connection was solid enough to act on. The second was what acting on it looked like in practical terms.

She had told him the connection was solid. She had told him that acting on it was a question she needed more time with.

James had said he would be there when she had the answer.

She had believed him.

***

She was corresponding with her father.

Through the custodian family in England, the same channel the letters had always used, moving at the pace that international physical correspondence moved, which was slow and certain and had a quality that the speed of digital communication did not produce, the quality of words that had been written and sealed and trusted to a physical process and that arrived carrying the specific weight of everything that had happened between the writing and the receiving.

She had received one letter from him since she sent hers.

She had read it three times and had not yet written in her notebook about what it said because some things needed more time before they were ready to be put into the shorthand of documentation. What she could say was that the letter confirmed what the six sentences had confirmed and opened questions that the six sentences had not addressed and that she was sitting with those questions in the patient way she had learned to sit with things that were not ready to resolve.

She was not ready to meet him.

She knew this about herself with the specific clarity that came from having examined the question honestly rather than from the angle of what she thought she should feel about it. Not yet. There was an order to things and they were both finding it and the order required more correspondence before it required presence and she was honoring that requirement not because someone had told her to but because she understood it.

He was in Peru. The sites were stable. The network she had been rebuilding was more connected than it had been in decades. There was time.

She thought about that often. About the specific gift of there being time. About what it meant to have found what she had found and to be in the position of approaching it carefully rather than desperately. Her mother had spent thirty-plus years protecting something without knowing the full scope of what she was protecting. Her father had spent twenty-three years monitoring something he could not be present for. Emma had time and tools and the full picture and the people around her who understood what she was doing and why.

She was not going to waste that by moving faster than the situation required.

***

It was a Tuesday morning in November when she walked to Carnegie Hall.

The November light on Main Street, the specific quality of late autumn Indiana light, lower and cleaner than the summer light she had been working by for months, casting the familiar buildings in a clarity that summer's warmth obscured. The hardware store open. The diner visible through its windows with the particular warm quality of a room that was full of people in the morning. Carnegie Hall's bell tower against the November sky, the floodlights off in the daylight, the stone of it unchanged and permanent and exactly where it had always been.

She pushed through the front door.

The cool interior. The smell of the building that she had been aware of her entire life, stone and age and the accumulated presence of a building that had been serving a community since 1907 and that had in its basement a ceremonial space that predated the building by more than five thousand years.

She went to her east window table.

Rufus settled under it. His chin on her foot.

She opened her laptop and opened her custodian notebook and looked at the name she had written three weeks ago with its single underline and then looked at the window and Carnegie Hall's bell tower and Main Street and the November morning going about its business outside.

She thought about what the name meant and what it required and what came next.

The custodian network was more complete than it had been in generations. The seven sites were stable and connected and maintained by families who understood what they were maintaining. The seal on the Carnegie Hall site was intact. The knowledge that had been nearly lost was not lost. It was here, in this building, in this notebook, in the people she had found and the connections she had built and the work that was not finished but was further along than it had been when she came back to Moores

Hill two years ago to figure out what her mother had been protecting.

She had figured out what her mother had been protecting.

She was protecting it now.

The name in the notebook with its single underline. Someone who had a foot in both worlds. Someone who had access to the custodian network's financial architecture and to the Safety Coalition's surviving infrastructure and who was, at this specific moment in November in the year after the grid went dark, unknown and unidentified and operating in the space between two things that were supposed to be opposed to each other.

Emma picked up her pen.

She opened the notebook to the page after the underlined name and began to write.

Not the name. What she knew about the name and what she did not know and what finding out what she did not know was going to require and who she was going to need to help her require it.

James. Owen. Clue-Minati Investigative Services, LLC, temporarily operating out of Moores Hill, Indiana, in the basement of a building that had been standing since 1907 above a ceremonial space that had been here since before recorded history.

She wrote until the morning light through the east windows had moved to midmorning light and Rufus had shifted twice beneath the table and the investigation had taken its first complete shape on the pages of the custodian notebook in the handwriting she had been developing for two years into the private notation of someone who was doing work that mattered and who intended to keep doing it.

She closed the notebook.

She looked at Carnegie Hall's bell tower through the east windows.

She thought about her mother. About thirty-plus years of protection sustained by instinct. About the letter in the attic that had started everything. About the ash circles in the basement below her and the inscription she had found and what it had meant and what it still meant and what it was going to mean for as long as the sites needed someone to stand between them and the people who wanted to destroy them.

She was the custodian of Moores Hill.

She had faced her shadow and said yes to the truth of herself.

She picked up her phone and called James.

He answered on the first ring.

"I'm ready," she said.

"I'll be right there," he said.

She set the phone down and looked at the notebook and looked at the bell tower and felt the particular quality of a beginning that had been building for a very long time and had finally arrived at the moment of its own readiness.

Outside Carnegie Hall, Moores Hill went about its November morning. The town that had been through something significant and was still standing, carrying the evidence of what it had been through in ways that were not always visible but that were always present.

Inside, Emma Caldwell waited for her partner.

The Patron was next.

The work was never finished.

That was exactly as it should be.

NOTES:

A Note on the Real Communities

St. Leon, Dover, New Alsace, and Yorkville are real places.

They sit in Dearborn County in southeastern Indiana, a few miles east of the I-74 corridor, the kind of communities that appear briefly on highway signs and are otherwise invisible to the people passing through. Family farms. Legion halls. Church suppers. The particular deep-rooted quality of places where the same last names appear on mailboxes and high school trophy cases and cemetery headstones across several generations.

The interchange at St. Leon is real. The overpass is real. SR 1 crosses I-74 exactly as described in Chapter 12. I drove it. East Central High School -- home of the Trojans -- is my alma mater.

The people in Chapter 12 -- the Bischoff brothers, Karl Schuman, Bill Steinmetz, Carol Kraus, the Zimmer family, Beau Hornbach -- are perhaps fictional. But they were built from the grain of the real communities they represent. The courage they demonstrate in that chapter is not the dramatic courage of extraordinary people in extraordinary circumstances. It is the ordinary courage of people who know each other, who have eaten chicken dinners together in the same hall for decades, and who do not leave when leaving is an option.

The research is consistent on this point. Communities with strong social networks and existing relationships of trust outperform larger populations in prolonged crisis scenarios by a significant margin. What Karl Schuman and the people of those four communities demonstrate in this novel is not a fantasy of rural virtue. It is a documented behavioral pattern of small communities under sustained pressure.

If you live in St. Leon, Dover, New Alsace, or Yorkville, or if you know someone who does -- this chapter was written in respect for what the people in those communities would actually do. I believe that without reservation -- and FEMA believes this too.

THE MOORES HILL THRILLER SERIES

TRILOGY ONE -- THE DISCOVERY

Book 1 -- **The Keeper**

A Moores Hill Thriller

Emma Caldwell returns to Moores Hill after her mother's death and discovers that the town she grew up in is protecting a secret older than the country itself. Emma has believed her father dead since she was eight years old. What she finds in Moores Hill will force her to question everything she thought she knew about her family and the ground she grew up on. The first book in the Discovery trilogy introduces Emma, Deputy James McClanahan, and a mystery that runs deeper than either of them is prepared for.

Book 2 **The Benefactor**

A Moores Hill Thriller

A stranger arrives in Moores Hill with resources and an agenda Emma cannot immediately read. The network of custodians that protects the sacred sites is larger than Emma understood -- and more fractured. The second book deepens the mythology and raises the stakes of what Emma has inherited.

Book 3 -- **The Custodian**

A Moores Hill Thriller

The full weight of the Custodian lineage falls on Emma as external threats converge on the Carnegie Hall site. Book 3 completes the Discovery trilogy and sets in motion the events that will define the second trilogy. The Ash-Craft families of Moores Hill remember more than they know.

TRILOGY TWO -- THE NETWORK

Book 4 -- **The Marked**

A Moores Hill Thriller

A regional grid failure pulls the power from half the Midwest and forces Emma Caldwell to investigate her father's past using only what she can find with her own hands. The fourth book opens the Network trilogy with dual point-of-view narration between Emma and James as the world they thought they understood goes dark around them.

Books 5 and 6 -- Coming

A WORD FROM THE AUTHOR

If you made it this far, you finished the book. That matters more to me than I can easily explain.

I spent thirty years as a Chief Information Security Officer and a VP of Global Data Centers. I spent those decades inside the infrastructure that the rest of the world takes for granted -- the systems that carry the power and the data and the communications that make modern life possible. I knew how fragile it was. I knew because I was paid to know, because knowing was the job, because the consequences of not knowing were things I was responsible for preventing.

When I sat down to write The Keeper, I did not intend to write a series about a grid failure. I intended to write a small-town thriller about a woman coming home to bury her mother and finding something she did not expect to find. The infrastructure story arrived later, as the world I was building demanded a crisis proportional to the themes I was exploring.

What I found when I started researching the grid failure scenario is documented in the Author's Note at the front of this book. I will not repeat it here. What I will say is that the research changed how I think about the communities in this series -- not just Moores Hill, but the communities surrounding it, the ones that most Americans drive past on the interstate without stopping.

Chapter 12 is the chapter I am most proud of in this book. Not for the writing, though I hope the writing serves the material. For what it says about ordinary people under extraordinary pressure, which is the only thing this series has ever really been about.

The people of small communities in this country are not waiting to be rescued. They are not the passive beneficiaries of decisions made somewhere else by someone else. When the conditions arrive that require them to be something more than what their ordinary lives demand, the research is consistent: they find a way.

I believe that. I wrote this series because I believe it.

The next book in the series is in progress. Emma and James are not finished, not even close.

Ray Brown
Human Perimeter Press
Moores Hill, Indiana -- May 2026

STAY CONNECTED

The themes in this series -- infrastructure vulnerability, surveillance capitalism, the erosion of privacy, and the resilience of small communities -- are not fictional concerns. They are the documented reality of the infrastructure we all depend on and the political economy that has grown up around it.

The Citizen Defense Movement is the non-fiction companion to this work. It is a place for people who finished a book like this one and wanted somewhere to take the concern it produced. You will find research, resources, and a community of people asking the same questions.

CitizenDefenseMovement.com

If this book found you through Amazon and you want to follow the series, the single most useful thing you can do is leave an honest review. Reviews are the primary way independent authors reach new readers. A few sentences from someone who finished the book is worth more than any advertising.

The Moores Hill Thriller Series is available wherever books are sold.

mooreshillthrillers.com

Human Perimeter Press -- Okeana, Ohio

www.ingramcontent.com/pod-product-compliance
Lightning Source LLC
LaVergne TN
LVHW100523110826
845146LV00002B/754

* 9 7 9 8 9 9 3 9 7 7 6 6 9 *